BOUGHT FOR HER BABY

Taken for her body...and her baby!

These men always get what they want—and the women who produce their heirs *will* be their brides!

Look out for all of our exciting books this month:

The Marciano Love-Child
Melanie Milburne

Desert King, Pregnant Mistress
Susan Stephens

The Italian's Pregnancy Proposal
Maggie Cox

Blackmailed for Her Baby
Elizabeth Power

Only from Harlequin Pres[illegible]TRA!

ELIZABETH POWER was born in Bristol, U.K., where she still lives with her husband in a three-hundred-year-old cottage. A keen reader, as a teenager she had already made up her mind to be a novelist. But it wasn't until a few weeks before her thirtieth birthday, when Elizabeth realized she had been telling herself she would "start writing tomorrow" for at least twelve of her first thirty years that she took up writing seriously. A short while later, the letter that was to change her life arrived from Harlequin. *Rude Awakening* was to be published in 1986. After a prolonged absence, Elizabeth is pleased to be back at her keyboard again, with new romances already in the pipeline.

Emotional intensity is paramount in Elizabeth's books. She says, "times, places and trends change, but emotion is timeless." A powerful storyline with maximum emotion, set in a location in which you can really live and breathe while the story unfolds, is what she strives for. Good food and wine come high on her list of priorities, and what better way to sample these delights than by having to take another trip to some new, exotic resort? To find a location for the next book, of course!

BLACKMAILED FOR HER BABY

ELIZABETH POWER

~ BOUGHT FOR HER BABY ~

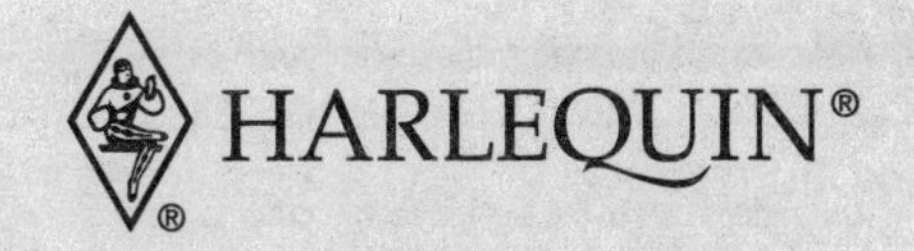

TORONTO • NEW YORK • LONDON
AMSTERDAM • PARIS • SYDNEY • HAMBURG
STOCKHOLM • ATHENS • TOKYO • MILAN • MADRID
PRAGUE • WARSAW • BUDAPEST • AUCKLAND

ISBN-13: 978-0-373-82366-6
ISBN-10: 0-373-82366-5

BLACKMAILED FOR HER BABY

First North American Publication 2008.

This edition published by arrangement with Harlequin Books S.A.

www.eHarlequin.com

Printed in U.S.A.

BLACKMAILED FOR HER BABY

CHAPTER ONE

'ONE more take, Blaze! That's it! Toss back that glorious mane of yours and smile. Smile up at the child. She's your daughter, remember. Higher! Lift her higher! Perfect! That's beautiful, darling! Bea-u-ti-ful!'

The gushing praise from the cameraman was as synthetic, Libby thought, as the relationship between herself and the giggling baby suspended high above her head. Like the nickname someone had given her at the outset of her career that had helped propel her up the ladder to supermodel status following a chance discovery at a small fashion show she had paraded in for a local charity.

What did it matter to the Press and the public that she was weary of pretending? That behind the shining trademark of her heavy red hair, the clothes and make-up and the pure artifice in standing in a summer meadow, promoting an exclusive range of skincare, which purported to make her skin as soft as that of any baby's, she was still just Libby Vincent. Or rather Vincenzo, she thought with a pained mental grimace. An average girl from an average background, who couldn't run away from who she really was no matter how hard she tried, or from the far from average burden of guilt she carried everywhere.

'OK! That's it! Beautiful, darling. Perfect!'

With an indiscernible sigh, she brought her arms down and the child with them, mercifully relieved that the shoot was over. She didn't think she could have endured another second.

The snowy fabric of her peasant skirt brushed her slender calves as she trudged back through the long grass. The baby she was reluctantly cradling crooned up at her, revealing two small white teeth, its little button nose wrinkling as it grasped her camisole with one tiny pink hand.

Libby dragged air through her lungs, a longing of such intensity sweeping over her that for an endless moment she couldn't seem to breathe as she fought the urge to clasp the infant fiercely to her.

Keeping a tight rein on her galloping emotions, her flawless features rigid as stone, somehow she made it back to the mobile make-up unit, where the rest of the team were waiting.

'Here.' The emotion clogging her throat made her sound decidedly curt as she thrust the child towards its mother, while the baby, obviously sensing the tension in Libby, began to bawl, her eager little arms outstretched as the other woman took her, leaving Libby to spin determinedly away.

'Isn't she a cutie?' Fran, a mature brunette with two growing boys of her own, couldn't help drooling as Libby approached, seeking only the seclusion of the huge green trailer behind them.

Beneath the make-up that Fran had applied so expertly earlier, Libby's face felt like a tight, tense mask. 'If you say so.'

'You'd forgotten, Fran.' It was the cynical voice of Steve Cullum, one of the technicians who had once asked Libby out and received the same polite brush-off for which she was renowned with the opposite sex. 'Blaze doesn't *do* maternal. Or any other sort of relationship for that matter.'

It was something the Press often speculated about. Her past. The lack of men in her life. Even, at times, her sexuality.

"Beneath the fire, is there only ice?" one tabloid newspaper had printed after she had refused to give them an interview, share with them her views on love, on marriage, on children.

And why should she? she thought bitterly now. These things

were private. Which was why, unsurprisingly, they had never found out her real name, never been able to connect her with Luca.

Anguish speared her as she thought about the boy she had married; about the tragic waste of life when he'd been killed in that car accident less than a year later. She had loved Luca; had had plenty of thoughts and feelings then. But that was a long time ago, before her emotions had been numbed by events and actions that were too damning even to think about; when loving had come naturally and she'd believed that happiness was everyone's birthright—even hers.

Inwardly she ridiculed herself for her gross naïvety. Because of course that was before she had met the prejudice and disapproval of the Vincenzo family. Before she'd felt his father's tyranny; known the cutting censure of Luca's darkly commanding older brother.

A prickly sensation lifted the hairs on the back of her neck as the disturbing features of Romano Vincenzo reared up before her eyes. A man who was lethally attractive and ruthlessly uncompromising. A man definitely not to be crossed. It hadn't just been mutual dislike that she had shared with Romano Vincenzo. It had been something more. Something much stronger and intensely profound that she had never been able to put a name to, and which she certainly wasn't going to waste any time wondering about six years on.

It was all in the past, and over the years she had become adept at hiding her emotions, which she did now, crushing her unwelcome reverie beneath a bright smile as Fran asked, 'Are you coming to the party tonight, Blaze?'

'You try and stop me!' It was a first-rate performance she was giving and she knew it; knew also that it was one she would have to keep up until she could change, get back to the Porsche and slam out of there, away from the turmoil of her unwelcome thoughts; of memories—resurrected by a simple skin-cream commercial—which she couldn't bear to face. 'After a week of staying in every night, getting up at four am and coming here to be bitten by mosquitoes,' she forced out laughingly over her shoulder, 'I'm going to party till dawn!'

* * *

Well, what had he been expecting? Romano thought, standing there in the trailer, when Libby, not looking where she was going, almost collided with him. That she had changed?

He caught her small gasp, felt her warmth and closeness and the pure femininity of her washing over him on a sensual wave.

'Buon giorno, Libby.' His senses, normally so controlled, were leaping into overdrive, making his heart race, his voice take on a husky quality as he watched the colour drain from the smooth texture of her high, Slavic cheekbones, saw her lush red mouth open in a gesture of pure shock.

'I'm sorry, Blaze…' Fran's voice followed her in, quickly contrite, breaking in on the whirling chaos of her thoughts. 'I meant to tell you. I'm sorry, Mr Vincenzo…' The woman's tone had changed in deference to the tall, tanned Italian hunk looming there in the aperture of her mobile studio and whose dark designer suit couldn't conceal the hard masculinity of the man beneath. 'I hadn't forgotten you were waiting…'

Romano's sleek black hair gleamed like jet as he gave a curt nod before reaching around the stunned Libby and pulling the trailer's sliding door closed with a rattling firmness that blocked out Fran and the rest of the world.

He hadn't changed, some small functioning part of Libby silently acknowledged. A high-profile entrepreneur, with that overall impression of lithe fitness and impeccable style, he still dominated any room he happened to walk into, still held sway over others with that bred-in-the bone confidence and effortless authority.

'Wh-what are *you* doing here?' Struck by the ridiculous notion that her thoughts must have conjured him up, Libby found herself as she'd always been in this man's company, a mixture of tongue-tied nervousness and challenging rebellion. And then, as shock receded and rational thought took over, she was urging in a voice strung with blind panic, 'What's wrong? What is it? Is something the matter?'

Some racing emotion darkened the long green eyes gazing up

at him from beneath their rich mahogany lashes as they had done from the covers of countless glossy magazines over the years.

'Not that I know of.'

He saw her eyes close, the pressing of those long, feathery lashes against the alabaster skin a response he understood and accepted, though not without a measure of surprise.

'How long have you been here?' Weak-kneed with relief—from this unexpected encounter with Luca's brother—Libby tried to get a grip on her errant thoughts.

'Long enough.'

His deeply-accented voice was as rich as she remembered it, his face as hard-boned and as classically structured, from his high intellectual forehead, straight nose and that forceful, darkly shadowed jaw to those penetrating black eyes that had always seemed to probe right down into the depths of her soul.

Her nostrils flaring, guardedly she demanded, 'Why didn't you make yourself known?'

His wide masculine mouth compressed, a mouth that could curl with disdain or make a woman's bones melt in the blaze of one smile. 'And miss watching the nation's loveliest model playing at doting motherhood?'

His double-edged compliment hit home hard and she swept determinedly past him, the brush of his jacket as their shoulders collided sending a tingling friction across her bare skin.

She gave a nonchalant little shrug, her feelings held on a throttle-tight leash. 'It isn't a role I'd normally have chosen.' In fact she had tried to refuse the job, but it was her agent who had warned her of the inadvisability of turning down such opportunities and who had won in the end.

Something flickered in Romano's eyes beneath his midnight-black lashes.

'Is that why you handed the kid over like she was a sack of potatoes?'

'Did I?' It was hard trying to pretend he wasn't unsettling her when even to her own ears her voice was shaking. 'I thought I was being careful.'

The firm mouth tugged downwards. 'As careful as you were when you handed over Giorgio?'

'Giorgi?' The name escaped her like a helpless little plea. He'd said there was nothing wrong, but something had to be because in all these years he had never chosen to patronise her with so much as a social call. 'He's all right, isn't he?'

It was only a heartbeat before he answered, and yet it seemed an eternity.

'That hasn't worried you for the past six years. So why should it suddenly concern you now?'

She couldn't tell him how much she had grieved for the baby son she had been forced to hand over so cruelly; how much she ached to see him, know him, her concern for his welfare and her need to be with him an excruciating pain that tore at her constantly no matter how many days, weeks, months or years dragged by.

'You wouldn't be here if it didn't concern Giorgio,' Libby breathed, feeling like a slave begging for mercy from a powerful master who held the key, not just to her happiness, but also to her very existence on this earth. 'Are you going to tell me what it is?' Her eyes were dark pools against the pale oval of her face. 'Or are you taking some sort of warped satisfaction out of seeing me suffer?'

'Suffer?' A thick eyebrow arched darkly against his tanned forehead. 'You? I don't think so, Libby. A moment ago you had nothing on your mind but partying until dawn.'

Libby felt something snap inside of her and the next moment, to her own horror, she was flying at him, fingers clamping like angry claws onto the expensive cloth of his jacket, her teeth clenched in an agony of frustration.

'Are you going to *tell* me? Or am I going to have to rip it out of you?' she sobbed, suddenly all too conscious of his physicality and the sheer power of him, the knowledge that he could subdue her with just one gram of his latent strength should he choose to do so.

Fortunately he didn't. Instead he caught her angry hands and held them against his chest, bringing her startlingly alive to the hard warmth of him beneath the impeccable cut of his clothes.

Some hot emotion burned in the incredibly dark gaze resting on her lips, strangely at odds with the deepening furrow between his eyes. 'Easy. Take it easy,' he advised hoarsely.

If he was truthful with himself, Romano thought, he was shocked by the strength of her reaction to what had, after all, been his unprovoked taunts. But what human being wouldn't feel justified in making them? he vindicated himself with his jaw clenching. Knowing exactly what made this single-minded little opportunist tick? But perhaps that was the reason for her wild and totally unexpected outburst. Guilt, it occurred to him suddenly. She'd be less than human if what she had done hadn't left her with some measure of remorse, so perhaps she *had* suffered. Because she *was* human, and very much a woman, two aspects he was vitally aware of now as he became conscious of the slender bones of her wrists beneath the hard pressure of his fingers, felt the life that was pulsing through her like the fluttering of a frantic sparrow so that he had to harden his swerving convictions and try to focus on her as the heartless little gold-digger she had proved herself to be, because he could deal with that.

'So there's a flame beneath the fire,' he recognised mockingly, obviously wise to that unkind headline about her. 'But then we always suspected I'd be the one to bring it out in you, didn't we, *cara*?'

'Wh-what are you talking about?' Libby stammered. He couldn't have the slightest notion of the way he had used to affect her—still affected her!—could he? she wondered hectically. Couldn't have guessed how he had plagued her troubled dreams even when she was happily married to his brother. But that was only because she had been so young, so overawed and intimated by him, she exonerated herself. Because she had loved Luca! She still loved Luca!

And Giorgio…

Her green eyes clouded over now as fear and grief, despair and a repression of feelings that she wasn't equipped to deal with coalesced with her maternal longing so that she swayed unsteadily under the weight of them.

'I think you'd better sit down.'

Catching his husky recommendation, shockingly aware of one iron-strong arm across her back, Libby did as she was told, dropping down onto the chair angled away from the mirror and Fran's pots of creams, mascara wands and lipstick phials.

Rocking back on his heels, Romano dragged in a deep breath. She wasn't going to like hearing what he had to say.

Wedging her hands between her knees to stop them trembling, Libby stared up at him as though he had just descended from a cloud.

'Would you mind repeating that?' she whispered.

His features were passive, his eyes hard and assessing. 'I think you heard me, Libby.'

Yes, she had, she realised, stunned, disbelieving. She hadn't yet come to terms with the fact that Romano Vincenzo was actually here—on the shoot—let alone got her brain round the demands he was suddenly making. In a minute, she thought, she would wake up and find that this was all some crazy dream, yet contrarily she knew he was anything but a figment of her imagination.

Here in this superficial world she inhabited, where everyone called her 'Blaze' and no one cared a jot for her beyond how well she could pretend to love the product they wanted to sell, he was the only representation of anything real; of her past, of which he was a vital part; of Luca and the girl she had once been. Only *he* knew who she really was. Or thought he did, she corrected bitterly.

'You want me to go to Italy with you?'

To see Giorgio…

She had never once expected that any member of the Vincenzo family would allow her to do that, let alone insist upon it.

She was trembling so much that she had to do something—anything—so she got up, moving like an automaton over to the couch where she had left her own clothes. Mindlessly, she started to peel off the skirt she had worn for the commercial with fingers that shook.

Watching his brother's widow, Romano couldn't believe how calmly she could carry on functioning as though he had said nothing, his eyes dark, judgemental slits in the hard lean, structure of his face.

Coldly he regarded the way the virginal fabric slithered down her long, golden legs, pooled alluringly around her ankles, the way she stepped nimbly out of it in nothing but her lacy white camisole and briefs.

'Had it been left to me I would never have entertained the thought of coming here,' he stated with grim assurance. 'I did so only because of a five-year-old who can't understand why it is that he doesn't have a mother. Who's trying to make sense of what it is he's done wrong.'

Libby choked back a small stifled cry as Romano continued, deaf and blind to how he was hurting her.

'A kid who's so distressed at being goaded by his peers he doesn't want to go to school any more. Won't sleep. Won't eat properly. Won't even play with his friends.' A five-year-old going on six who couldn't be placated with a new pony or a trip to Disneyland. Who foolishly believed his Zio Romano could make anything happen—including bringing home the mother who didn't want him!

The child had been pushing him and pushing him until Romano—always able to solve the most intricate problems in his multi-faceted business empire—didn't know what else to do. His trusting nephew. A bright, intelligent kid. Luca's son.

He hadn't realised just how many problems the boy had until recently. His mother had been right, though, he accepted grudgingly. His father would never have let Libby Vincent—as he'd recently discovered she called herself—near his grandson. That was if she had ever entertained any desire to see Giorgio, which he strongly doubted. The demands of a growing, energetic youngster would simply have put paid to her shallow, artificial life!

She was tugging off her camisole and, unable to help himself, Romano gazed broodingly at the willowy arc of her raised arms as she pulled it over her head, at the smooth, golden contours of her slender back.

Her skin was the texture of silk, her tapering waist amazingly small above the gentle flare of her hips. Unashamedly, as she turned slightly, his gaze flickered upwards to the outer curve of one beautifully shaped breast and desire kicked him in the loins, making his breath lock beneath the hard cage of his ribs.

She was a model. Just a face and body to promote whatever lucrative opportunities came her way. She was used to undressing in front of others. Yet now, as he found himself resenting every other man who must have seen her like this, he realised that her power to ensnare was as strong and as lethal to him now as it had ever been.

Because he had been bewitched by this girl! Had fallen under her spell from the first moment he had met her and she had fixed him with those proud yet wary emerald eyes. Wary, because she had known at once that he could see right through her; recognise—just as his parents had—what a scheming little gold-digger she was.

And yet that still hadn't stopped him wanting her—stopped him envying Luca—or from lying awake at night, mentally beating himself up for allowing himself to become totally captivated by his younger brother's wife.

She had appeared like a breath of spring in a jaded world, possessing a quiet maturity that went way beyond her years. But that cultivated innocence that was the other side of the coin—and which sometimes almost roused in him a ludicrous desire to protect—hadn't fooled him. She was as heartless as he'd believed her to be—and as mercenary.

She was pulling on a cheesecloth shirt, for which he was extremely grateful, because even the reminder of what this girl was really like couldn't cool the fierce desire she aroused in him, more strongly now, if that were possible, than she had in the past.

Tensely Libby fumbled with the buttons of her shirt, glaringly self-conscious of the way Romano had been looking at her ever since she'd unthinkingly pulled off her clothes. As if he wanted to wrench the rest from her body, she realised, with heat tingling along her nerve-endings, reawakening her to the frightening power of his sexuality.

'My son is giving you problems and your family suddenly decides it wants to invite me back into its oh-so-loving circle!' Her injured little statement was strung with all the bitterness she had harboured towards the Vincenzo family since she had been a vulnerable and powerless teenager.

'Not the family,' he negated tersely. 'My mother is against it. And my father—as I'm sure you must know—is dead.'

Yes, she knew that. It had made all the papers six months ago. The demise of a man as wealthy as Marius Vincenzo didn't go unreported. There had been a piece about Romano too. It was that that she had soaked up with the thirst of someone parched while knowing that they were drinking from a poisoned well. It had been a brief account of how an important area of Vincenzo-held interests—once floundering under Marius Vincenzo—had started to flourish again when his son had taken over to pull it out of stormy waters and, with his head for business and fearless judgement, shares had rocketed now that he was fully in command. His achievements really were quite remarkable. Since the demise of Luca's grandfather, there was no doubt among the Vincenzo males where the real influence and talents really lay.

'I'm sorry,' she uttered curtly, experiencing a pang of guilt because she couldn't feel any regret. Marius Vincenzo had been a tyrant and she had disliked him more than it was possible to dislike anyone. 'For you, that is,' she felt she had to add, because it wasn't in her nature to be hypocritical. 'And your mother,' eventually she decided to tag on.

Sophia Vincenzo hadn't liked her, any more than her overbearing husband had. In fact the only thing she had had in common with her rather frosty-tongued mother-in-law was that they had both loved Luca. A love that had festered hatred on the woman's part towards Libby after the death of the woman's favourite and idolised younger son.

The light from the high windows of the trailer emphasised the hard lines around Romano's mouth as he dipped his head, acknowledging her. Her condolences had surprised him though. She had had as little time for his parents as they had had for each other, he thought cynically, remembering the farce of a united front his parents had shown to the world.

'Well, then,' Libby accepted pointedly, telling herself not to get too excited, hope for too much, though every cell was leaping from even the smallest chance of seeing her son again. 'If your mother's against it, there's little more to be said, is there? After all, she's his guardian.'

'No.'

That incisive response brought Libby's gaze flying to his. He was so big and darkly dominating in the confined area of the trailer that she could feel him, touch him, breathe him in almost, his lethally magnetic presence with the subtle spice of the cologne he used infiltrating the space around them, percolating the very air she needed to fill her lungs.

'My mother's too weary these days to cope with an energetic child. I'm the boy's official guardian now.'

'But I thought…' Libby's words tailed off. How could it be possible? Her son. Her baby. In the care of Romano Vincenzo? The man who had made his distrust of her felt in the way his parents had never done. Subtly and with a hard-edged intelligence that had hurt even more because, surprisingly, there had been odd times when he had shown snatches of consideration towards her.

'You thought what, Libby?' His hard mouth twisted with bitter derision. 'That he'd be handed over to someone else? Packaged off as just a nuisance? In the way?'

As he thought she had packaged him off when Luca had died?

'So you see, *cara*,' he said with a controlled softness that sent shivers through her yearning insides, 'whatever you decide to do, or how you act or decide to treat my nephew, you're only answerable to me. Well?'

One thick eyebrow moved questioningly as she reached for her jeans. She could sense his eyes following her every movement as she pulled them on, hips moving with unintentional sensuality in her keenness to wriggle into them, her breath quickening from what he might be thinking, and from the sudden reckless speculation of what it would be like to have those long, dark hands shaping every curve of her lissom frame.

'Well what?' she challenged acridly, pushing the fitted shirt into her waistband, her movements agitated from the outrageous and unwelcome images that had suddenly invaded her mind. 'I come back and fill the gap in Giorgio's life until you suddenly decide you don't need me any more?' She couldn't bear that. Didn't think she could cope with the heartache of parting from him again once she had been allowed to play even a small part in his life. And yet she would! she resolved desperately. No matter how much it cost her emotionally, she would do it! Just to see him. Be with him again. Hold him in her arms, if only for the shortest time.

'It's Giorgio who needs you,' Romano reminded her coldly. 'I, fortunately, have been spared that particular privation.'

His words stung, as he'd intended them to.

'Have you really?' It was a shrill little retaliation as she battled not to give him the satisfaction of knowing it. Proudly she faced him with her head held high. Yet now, as her eyes clashed with the glittering depths of his, she was shocked to recognise the familiar desire she'd become accustomed to seeing in the eyes of nearly every man she met, only with this man she could tell it was a dark obsession for which he despised himself.

Way down inside her something throbbed. Some equally dark emotion she didn't want to acknowledge.

'Why do you hate me so much, Romano?' For all her maturity her voice still quavered as that eighteen-year-old's had done. 'Is it because you hold me responsible for Luca's death?'

His features seemed to darken from a well of repressed emotion. Clearly it still hurt to talk about the brother who had been six years his junior.

'I've never blamed you for that.'

'Well, bravo!' Libby's head came up in a toss of flaming cynicism. 'Why not? Your father did!'

'But I'm not my father!' He was only barely restraining a surprising degree of anger, as something in what she had said sent a surge of colour slashing across his hard-boned cheeks. A second later, however, and he was back in control, though his features were still rigid as he said with marked acceptance, 'Luca was careless in his driving that day—and he paid for it.' He saw a shadow cross her face, swift as a bird, leaving a crease between the fine arches of her velvety brows. 'And hate,' he said now, 'is rather too strong a word I'd use to describe any emotion I felt in connection with you. Hate is the flip-side of love—' his tone derided, his sharp eyes assessing her for every change of expression, the smallest chink in her wavering composure '—and I think we'd both agree that whatever else was bubbling under the surface of our relevant personalities, love certainly didn't come into it.'

Uncomfortably, Libby swallowed. However had they managed to get on to this?

Deciding though that he was merely trying to unsettle her, she ignored the prickly tension creeping through her to say, 'So if I did agree to what you're asking, what am I expected to do at the end of it all? When things improve? Just walk away?'

'That shouldn't be too difficult for you.'

Libby's breath seemed to catch in her lungs as his remark drove into her like an antagonist's spear.

'How do you know what would be difficult for me? How do you know what it's like? What it's ever been like for me?' she challenged, her flush deepening, her breasts rising and falling heavily from a long-buried anger that had no outlet, no hope of ever being assuaged.

'My heart bleeds for you,' he said, one long, tanned hand coming to rest on his ribcage. He knew only too well about women who gave up their babies for a better life!

'You don't have one!' From the little she had read about him, there didn't seem to be one woman among this very eligible billionaire's acquaintance who could keep him interested for more than a few months, let alone commit him to undying devotion to her!

He laughed without humour, long ebony lashes drooping, concealing the darkened depths of his beautiful eyes. 'That, *cara mia*, is rich coming from you. How much more heartless can you get than a woman who abandons her child?'

'I didn't abandon him!' Pain, raw and crushing propelled Libby to her feet. She could feel his contempt beating against her like a tangible thing. 'Anyway, I'm not the first woman ever to have had a baby adopted!'

'No, you're not the first by any means,' Romano agreed, disdain twisting his mouth as he delivered with hard incision, 'but it takes a certain kind of girl who can hand over her baby purely for cash!'

Libby felt as if she'd been hit in the solar plexus, the cruelty of his statement almost making her double up. She had to restrain a strong urge to punch her late husband's brother right back between his spectacular eyes.

He must, however, have seen the anguish corrugating her forehead because he said with quiet, yet unmistakable censure, 'It does sound rather distasteful, doesn't it?'

Raw with emotion, Libby couldn't answer. Nor could she get to grips with the fact that he could actually believe it.

'*Dio sa!* You don't deserve it, Libby. But I'm offering you the chance to make amends.'

'Make amends?' She looked at him obliquely, hot, angry tears smarting against her eyes. Just who did he think he was? Her judge and jury? 'How magnanimous of you!' she bit out, her defences in shreds. But, needing to ease the ever-present guilt, redeem herself in her own eyes if no one else's, she was crying out in bitter denial, 'I didn't *sell* my child!'

The firm masculine mouth tugged with grim scepticism. 'Find a way of telling that to Giorgio when he grows up.'

Pain darted across Libby's already tortured features, pale now against the rich red lustre of her hair. 'That surely isn't what you...what your parents...' She couldn't bring herself to finish. It was too awful even to contemplate that they might have said as much to the little boy.

'You think I'd be—' he broke off, his eyes hard '—let anyone be that cruel?'

A surge of relief lifted Libby's chest. Luca's brother might feel only contempt for *her*, but he did seem to have some sensitivity where Giorgio was concerned.

'I have evidence of it, Libby,' he went on in those deep, relentless, self-assured tones. 'You were paid...' He paused before spelling out the exorbitant sum of money that his father had drafted into her bank account on the handing over of her eight-week old son. 'And unless my accounts are well and truly—what is the expression?—up the creek—there isn't any doubt that all the money was cashed within a few months.'

Well, he owed me something! Libby wanted to scream, though nothing had, or ever could, compensate for, or ease the loss of her child.

'Yes, I cashed it,' she uttered vehemently, because she had no intention of explaining to this hard-headed Italian who had formed so many erroneous opinions about her what she had done with the money. He was a Vincenzo after all and, with the exception of Luca, just like the rest. 'I had to live.'

'*Si.*' There was only raw cynicism in his reply as his gaze fell on a back issue of a leading magazine someone had left on the cosmetics shelf. The cover featured a Ferrari with Libby draped over its gleaming red bonnet, dripping with the gold jewellery she had been advertising. 'And quite well if that fancy car you drive out there and that string of homes you appear to own besides your expensive London apartment are anything to go by. One in Jersey. A couple on the continent. Two beach houses in Florida. Not bad for a girl who started out without a bean to her name.'

No, she had all that, she accepted gratefully. But, just like with the money, it was none of his business, and she was darned if she'd be made to feel accountable to him for why she had invested in so many homes!

Her chin coming up, exposing the pale line of her throat, she said simply, 'Are you sure there isn't anything else you'd like to throw at me?'

His dark gaze plundered hers as though searching for something beyond their defensive green depths.

'I appreciate that you have commitments. That it isn't going to be easy for you to...drag yourself away.' Carefully chosen words, Libby felt, to make each statement a precision-aimed snipe. The lining of his jacket gleamed darkly as he reached for something in his inside pocket, the action exposing the dark shading of body hair through the fine material of his shirt. 'So name your price,' he invited silkily. 'I'm sure together we can come to a suitable figure.'

To see Giorgio? He thought she needed payment before she'd consider helping her son!

'How dare you?' She lashed out at the black leather folder he was opening, almost hitting it out of his hands. 'Get out! Get out of here if all you can do is stand there and sling insults at me!'

From the way his brows lifted, clearly her reaction had taken him unawares. His hands were remarkably steady, though, as he repocketed the offending cheque-book. 'Forgive me,' he said coldly. 'I forgot. These days Vincenzo money doesn't hold the same attraction for you that it did.'

'No, that's right,' Libby breathed, hating him more with every second that passed. If he wanted to think the worst about her, then let him think it! 'And as for my car and all my houses…I do have my image to think about!'

She thought he would come back with some further cutting remark, but all he did was stand there looking down at her for a few dissecting moments from his superior height.

Eventually he took something out of his wallet, handed it to her. A card with the familiar Vincenzo logo printed at the top. 'I'll be here in London for a couple of days, ' he stated in a cool, unperturbed voice. 'If you've a glimmer of conscience or compassion behind that beautiful face of yours—call me. It might do you good to step down into the real world for a while—see how the other half lives.'

His comments flayed as he pushed back the sliding door, his broad shoulders filling for a moment the gap he had created, before he stepped lithely down from the trailer and strode away.

Staring after his lean, elegant figure, Libby felt frustrated tears bite behind her eyes. The real world, he'd said. Was that what he called the Vincenzo mansion and its accompanying millions? When it was his and his family's world that had taught her how the other half lived! The half who could buy anything, threaten anything, just as long as they got exactly what they wanted, when they wanted it, regardless of who got hurt!

Her knuckles whitening as she gripped the open door, anguish a crushing weight in her chest, she almost gave in to the urge to call him back. Tell him that she would go to Italy with him. Now if he demanded it of her. Agree to anything he stipulated just so long as she could see Giorgio again. But he was already folding himself into the low sports saloon parked in front of her own favoured Porsche that he had spoken of so critically, and the next instant the powerful car was growling away.

Without even bothering to cream off her make-up, Libby packed up her few belongings and followed his example. The day, accommodatingly bright and cloudless for the shoot, was turning overcast as she headed back to the city and the rain had set in heavily before she had got very far. She tried to keep her mind on her driving, but even concentrating hard on the wet road through the double speed of the windscreen wipers couldn't keep the bitter memories at bay.

CHAPTER TWO

SHE had still been at college when she had met Luca Vincenzo.

Motherless, with her father pensioned off early through ill health, she had been waiting tables at weekends and during term holidays in a chic little bistro in the Sussex village where she lived, eager to contribute in whatever way she could to their frugal finances.

She couldn't deny that her unusually photogenic looks and striking red hair, which she accepted without a trace of vanity, helped to get her noticed with the customers, bringing in more than a fair share of tips from admiring male members of the clientele, from whom she always managed to pleasantly but firmly distance herself.

Luca had been the one exception to the rule. A handsome Italian boy with a daredevil attitude to life, he had dined there every night for a month, wooing her with his crazy Latin charm and that hint of devilry in his sparkling dark eyes until she took his threat of hiring a helicopter and lowering himself onto the top of Nelson's column, where he promised to stay until she put him out of his misery and agreed to go out with him, as serious. It was only after she had laughingly consented to that she discovered exactly who he was; what a wealthy, respected and—in his own words—stifling family he had been born into.

Braking to allow a van to pull across into her lane, she remembered how much her father had liked Luca. As he'd liked Luca's grandfather, Giovanni Vincenzo, she recalled fondly, whom he'd worked for, prior to his forced retirement, as head gardener on the man's large country estate fringing the village. When Giovanni Vincenzo had died, it was Luca's father, Marius, who inherited the family empire. Preferring to run his international enterprises from his native Italy, he had turned the house into a conference centre and country club and, with the exception of a few small properties, sold off the rest of the estate.

Earmarked for a responsible position in the family business, Luca had spent that summer getting experience at the conference centre that still remained in Vincenzo hands. At twenty-one and three years older than her, Luca had seemed like a man of the world, Libby thought, looking back. Well-travelled. Exciting. Although it was his warm humour and the feeling that he wasn't wholly appreciated by a family who wanted to curb his adventurous spirit that had endeared her to him. A family, she thought disparagingly now, who were far too busy multiplying its millions to take much interest in anything Luca wanted.

Head over heels in love, when he had asked her to marry him after only a few weeks she didn't even have to think about it, she remembered sadly, trying to focus on the road through the spray thrown up by the van in front of her. They had been married almost immediately in a small private ceremony in the local register office with only her father and another waitress from the bistro as witnesses. It had all seemed so exciting and romantic at the time. It wasn't until her new husband had taken her to meet his parents in their restored castle in Italy that she had realised how strongly they'd objected to Luca's marrying her. Regardless of her studies, she was just a part-time waitress with no money and no prospects, and in their eyes an opportunist and a gold-digger. Their unveiled coolness towards her could have been chipped at with an ice-pick, his mother's unrestrained remark privately to Libby that she had anticipated a far more suitable match for her son leaving Libby in no doubt as to exactly where she belonged. Anywhere but in the close-knit Vincenzo family circle!

As she steered her car through the slow-moving, increasingly heavy traffic, it still hurt to remember her in-laws' attitude towards her, even though she had tried desperately to win their respect. Because of the conditions his father had laid down, she had had plenty of opportunity. They were to live in the castle, he had stipulated unswervingly. Otherwise he would take it to mean that their son was no longer a Vincenzo.

Luca had been all for walking out, Libby recalled, until she had persuaded him against it. The last thing she had wanted was to be responsible for a break-up between her husband and his family.

'They'll come round. You'll see,' she had naïvely reassured him, unaware of how influencing him to stay only served to reinforce her in-laws' derogatory opinion of her. After all, she thought with cutting poignancy now, if she had allowed Luca to oppose his father she would have been walking away from the fortune he would have eventually inherited, wouldn't she?

The van in front of her stopped dead, causing her to ram on her brakes. Through her obscured vision she could just make out that there were traffic lights ahead.

Berating herself for her lack of concentration, she tried to steer her thoughts back to the present. But the floodgates of her past, blown apart by that earth-shattering visit from Romano, had unleashed a torrent of unwelcome memories and, now that they had free passage, nothing could stem the flow.

Romano had been working abroad, she remembered, when Luca had taken her to Italy, but had come home within a few days of their arrival, sent for, she was sure, to meet, vet and generally dissect his younger brother's new wife.

At twenty-seven, Romano Vincenzo had already been a powerful player in the family's global commercial empire. Where Luca was warm, witty and handsome, Romano Vincenzo was cold with a serious mind and an incisive intellect, linked with that raw animal attraction that transcended mere good looks. It wasn't just the hard structure of his face and that athletically built physique that made one notice him, Libby accepted resentfully, watching the rain streaming down the windscreen. It was everything about him—and he had it in bucketfuls. Presence. Personality. Poise.

Standing there in the castle's imposing drawing room, he had intimidated her from the first, asking her questions about herself, innocent enough on the surface but leaving her feeling as though he was testing her with every perfectly articulated syllable, while his richly accented English ran like honey off his well-trained, interrogative tongue! Consequently, nervous and awkward in his presence, she had cloaked herself in a confidence she was far from feeling.

Sometimes during that first trip home of his she'd glanced up to catch him watching her, the dark absorption in those penetrating eyes disturbing her as much as she was sure it had been his intention to, before he'd resumed whatever it was he had been doing and turned dispassionately away.

It was the day he was due to fly back to whatever area of the Vincenzo empire was calling him that stood out in her memory. Having said his goodbyes to the rest of the household, he had come out onto the terrace, where she had been emerging from the pool after seeking some relief from the strained atmosphere inside the house.

'It's been more than…interesting meeting you, Libby,' he'd told her silkily, his dark, executive image doing untold things to her equilibrium as she'd stood there in nothing but her skimpy bikini. 'In fact it's been rather remiss of me, but I do believe I haven't yet kissed my brother's new bride.'

She'd held herself rigid as he'd placed his hands on her wet shoulders, heart thumping against her ribcage, back stiffening in rejection as his lips impinged in no more than a brotherly gesture on her burning cheek.

'You claim to love Luca, but I think we both know differently, don't we?' he'd challenged with a menacing softness, his warm breath fanning her hair, his scent and sound and touch an assault on her screaming senses before he'd picked up the briefcase he'd set down on the tiles and stridden away.

Staring broodingly after his broad back, she had wondered if he'd sensed the way that simple gesture had made her blood race through her, and if he'd guessed at her mind's screaming rejection of the sensations that had ravaged her even from that briefest contact with him.

He probably thought he was irresistible to her! she remembered thinking hotly, because his ego was enormous enough and because, just like his parents, he believed that her interest in Luca lay only in what she could gain financially.

The incident, though, had unsettled her. Even remembering it now caused an icy little shiver to course down her spine. It was the cold realisation that it was entirely possible to love one man while still being shockingly aware of another—even if you didn't like him, she thought, grappling with the gear stick as an impatient hooting from the car behind jolted her into realising that the lights had changed. And she certainly hadn't liked Romano Vincenzo! The feelings he'd aroused in her had been irrational, born only out of a kind of warped fascination coupled with dislike, and nothing like the warm, tender feelings she'd shared with Luca.

On the move again, she recalled how elated she had been when she'd become pregnant almost immediately, and how her joy had been tempered by the sudden worrying turn of her father's health. With no one to look after him, she'd made frequent visits back to England, the long periods she'd spent caring for him instead of being in Italy with her husband adding yet another detrimental mark against her in her in-laws' eyes.

As she brought her car into the familiar tree-lined square, the memory of that time and everything that followed pressed down on her like a dark, suffocating cloud.

When she had gone into labour, unexpectedly here in England, given birth to a healthy baby boy, her life should have been complete. But it hadn't worked out that way, she reflected achingly.

Luca had had that accident rushing to the airport to be with her, and his parents, already despising her more than she could have believed possible, had no qualms about blaming her for his death. After all, if she'd been there where she belonged instead of abandoning her husband and her responsibilities, their son would still be alive, his mother had sobbed accusingly to her over the phone.

It was something Libby had been all too conscious of, but having it spelt out by someone else—someone who loved him just as much as she did—was almost too much to bear.

It was several weeks later when she'd gone back to Italy to collect a few of her and Luca's things that they had dropped their bombshell.

They wanted to adopt Giorgio. Bring him up as their own. Couldn't she see that the boy would have a far more privileged and stable upbringing with them than he would with a sick grandfather and a single mother? How could she allow their grandchild to be deprived of all they could offer him? How could she be that selfish? they had asked her when, horrified, she'd refused at first even to give any headroom to such an unthinkable idea. She'd wanted to look after her baby herself—*and* care for her father. She'd known there would be difficult times ahead, but she'd manage, she'd determined. Wouldn't she? After all, other girls did. It had continued to be impressed upon her, though, how selfish she was being. That she didn't have her child's interests at heart. Even her father had tentatively suggested that perhaps she ought to consider the Vincenzos' offer very carefully. She was young—had her whole life in front of her. Had she considered the enormity of what she was taking on?

Tortured and afraid, she had clung desperately to Luca's child. She could never give him up! She couldn't! Though the pressure to do so had been almost overwhelming, she might not have given in. Not if Marius Vincenzo, determined to wear down her resistance, hadn't come up with that cruel ultimatum…

Blindly, she left her car in the reserved parking bay outside the rank of exclusive Georgian apartments and, dodging the rain, raced up the steps, shutting her mind to the bitter choice the man had given her. She couldn't relive it—couldn't think about it now.

She only knew as she rode the lift up to the first floor—let herself into the welcoming haven of her own apartment—that when she had been forced to sign that piece of paper, handing over her son to Luca's family, she had been too young and too worried about her father to see beyond her naïve hopes in believing that one day she would get her baby back.

A persistent ringing of the doorbell had Libby reluctantly answering it. Since abandoning all thoughts of going out, she'd bathed and changed and she certainly didn't feel like seeing anyone tonight.

'Surprise!' Fran and about a dozen others carolled from the front doorway, before breezing in brandishing bottles of champagne.

'As it was obvious you weren't coming to the party, we decided to bring the party to you,' a young woman Libby didn't even recognise announced, her voice raised above the animated conversation and laughter.

'I can't. Really, I can't face this now,' Libby protested over the sound of corks already being popped, glasses being hauled out of her china cabinet. Someone had switched on her CD player, and a sea of bodies began gyrating to a deafening rhythm.

She wanted to scream at them to get out. After meeting Romano today there had been no question of attending the end of the assignment party. She had had a lot of decisions to make, appointments to cancel. On top of which her thoughts were in turmoil and her head was thumping.

'Are you all right?' Fran shouted to make herself heard above the noise.

'No, I'm not!' Libby yelled back. 'I just want to be alone!'

'You always do!' Fran's more mature features were contorted in friendly chastisement. 'We thought it would do you good not to let you get away with not turning up for yet *another* party. We thought… Hey! Are you OK?' The make-up artist looked genuinely concerned, but trying to compete with the din in her flat was hurting Libby's throat.

With a hopeless shrug she swept away from them all, towards the sanctuary of her bedroom.

'Everybody! Everybody! Blaze doesn't need this!' From behind the closed door, she heard Fran's futile attempts to make her protests heard. 'I really think we ought to go!'

Someone turned up the music. After a few moments the sound burst intrusively into the bedroom as the door opened and then closed again, admitting a penitent-looking Fran.

'I'm sorry, Blaze. I didn't realise,' the woman expressed, as Libby flopped limply down onto the bed. 'We really were only thinking of you. I tried.... What's this?' Fran's sudden diversion drew Libby's eyes to the single bed and the little white album lying on the coverlet that she hadn't had chance to put away. 'What is this?' The woman was picking it up, surveying the embossed gold lettering on the leather-bound cover and, despairingly, Libby saw her taking in the first two pages of photographs, then the subsequent blank white pages that told their own story. 'Am I imagining this…' the woman's puzzled gaze lifted from the few appealing baby photos to clash with Libby's '…or does he look like…?' Fran's voice tailed off, her mouth an open circle of disbelief. '*Yours?*' she whispered, dumbfounded.

Leaping up, Libby grabbed the incriminating album and snapped it shut. 'He belonged to someone else,' she said quickly, her voice noncommittal. Well, it was true, wasn't it? she thought achingly. And if it got out that she had married into the Vincenzo family—one of the richest families in Italy—was the mother of Luca Vincenzo's son, then because of her celebrity status Giorgio would be hounded by the Press, and his little life would cease to be his own.

Fran gave her a sidelong glance. 'Belonged?' she echoed gingerly and, when Libby said nothing, 'I'm sorry,' the woman sighed, guessing that something had gone terribly wrong in her young friend's life, but clearly didn't want to probe too deeply. 'You never said.'

Libby shrugged. 'It's in the past.' Only it wasn't. It never would be, she thought, speared with wanting. Giorgio was hers—part of the here and now—and all she wanted was for this rowdy uninvited crowd to leave so that she could ring the boy's uncle and tell him that she was ready to go with him. That she would throw in her job, her flat, and every commitment she'd made and leave now—this minute—with nothing but the clothes she stood up in just as long as she could see her baby again.

Hastily she stuffed the album into a drawer. 'Promise me you won't say anything to the others?'

'Of course not,' Fran uttered in compliance, and Libby didn't doubt that the woman would be as true as her word. 'Was there some connection with that gorgeous hunk who turned up on the shoot today? Did you have an affair with him or something?'

'No!' Fran knew that there was no man in her life, and that she didn't date, so an eye-catching specimen like Romano showing up would naturally arouse her curiosity.

'He seemed pretty possessive. The way he slung that door closed in my face. Only a lover behaves like that.'

'No!' Libby denied with a vehemence that had one of Fran's dark brows lifting in patent scepticism. Why would she think that? Libby thought angrily, guessing that while her friend knew when to let the subject of a lost child drop, the possibility of such a ruthlessly attractive male as Romano Vincenzo as a candidate for Libby's bed was too much even for the discreet Fran to ignore.

The music was still pounding away in the sitting room. Animated shouts with the rhythmic thud of feet reverberated through the apartment. Suddenly a loud banging was cutting insistently through the pandemonium.

'Your neighbours?' Fran suggested with a grimace.

'Oh, good grief!' If it was, then they had every right to complain. 'Help me get rid of this lot, will you?' Libby appealed despairingly to her friend.

'I will,' Fran promised, giving her an affectionate squeeze. 'After all, it was my fault you got stuck with…' Her words were drowned beneath a wall of sound as the bedroom door opened and the blond technician who had been on the shoot peered round it.

'Having a tête-à-tête?' His words were a little slurred, Libby noted, guessing that he had already been drinking heavily before he'd arrived and was clearly the worse for too much champagne. 'I thought for a moment the lovely Blaze had got herself a man in here, but I should have known better, shouldn't I?'

'Leave it, Cullum,' Fran advised, wiser now to what made Libby such a loner.

Steve Cullum, though, Libby noticed, looked aggressive enough to swing a punch at someone, and hurriedly she made to defuse the situation.

'Let's go back and join the others,' she suggested to him in a placatory tone, pushing him gently back into the other room so that she could go and answer the persistent thudding on her front door.

'Only if you'll dance with me.'

'All right. All right,' she promised recklessly. 'After I've answered the door to whoever's out there first.' Humour him. Don't be offensive, she warned herself, knowing from experience that it was the only way to handle drunks. 'Someone turn the music down!' she shouted, making a move towards the hall.

'Turn it up!' The technician was grabbing her arm, shouting at the top of his voice, 'Turn it up! Blaze wants to dance! Blaze wants to dance with *me*!'

Libby tried to resist as he spun her round in the middle of the floor and, with his arms crossing her chest, pulled her back against him, forcing her body to sway with his to the raucous music.

His aftershave lotion was cloying, and his alcohol-stained breath was revoltingly warm against her throat. Somewhere in her repulsed brain it registered that the banging on the front door had stopped. That the neighbour had given up all hope of being heard and gone—probably to call the police!

'Come on, baby, dance. You know how to move.' The scoop-necked sweater she had changed into when she'd showered had slipped off one shoulder and the man's mouth was suddenly moving, hot and moist, across her bare flesh. Trapped in his arms, she jerked her head aside, but he only laughed and tightened his hold on her.

In a minute, she decided, she was going to elbow him—hard!

The only thing that stopped her was the shocking silence as the music was cut dead, along with every other sound in the room.

All eyes were turned towards the CD player and the man in the impeccable dark raincoat and executive suit who was straightening up beside it. And it wasn't just the formality of his clothes but that hard air of command that set him apart from everyone else in the room.

Romano Vincenzo!

Stunned, Libby could only gaze speechlessly at his strong, tanned face and those glittering black eyes, which, focusing only on her now, flared, like those proud nostrils, with unequivocal anger.

'I think you'd better ask your friends to leave.' His recommendation fizzed with seething displeasure.

Barely able to grasp that it must have been him who had been thundering on the door—that someone had let him in—Libby could only despair at the compromising position in which he had walked in and found her, locked as she still was in the technician's arms. Things couldn't look worse, she thought, knowing that it wasn't the first time that he had caught her in a situation like this.

'Romano!'

It was all she could utter as Steve Cullum lifted his head to demand in a slurred voice, 'Are you suggesting I quit this party and walk out of here—just because you said so?'

Beneath his rain-splashed coat, Romano's shoulders squared. The last thing he wanted was trouble. But the sight of Libby, the girl who had plagued his thoughts and got under his skin as he had allowed no other woman to do—filling him with self-disgust when she was married to his brother—and who still aroused the same complexity of emotions in him—not only living it up after all he had told her today without a care for her child, which just went to prove just how heartless she was, but also crushed against that lecherous drunk, which she was obviously consenting to, only fuelled his anger, filling his veins with cold, jealous fury.

'That's exactly what I'm suggesting.' Anger blanched the skin around his taut upper lip. 'Unless you'd rather be thrown.'

Feeling the technician's body tightening up behind her, Libby sucked in a breath. The last thing she wanted to witness was a brawl. But one step forward from the man who was taller, broader and light-years ahead in the fitness stakes than the inebriated Steve Cullum had the technician instantly backing off.

'OK, mate. OK. Keep your shirt on.' Hands held up in acquiescence to the other man's dominant will, he moved grudgingly away, while the others, bottles in hand, their eyes fixed on Romano, also started filing out, muttering their goodnights to Libby as they yielded to an authority they recognised as one not to be tested.

'Still denying it?' Fran grimaced as she moved past Libby.

Denying what? Libby asked herself, quietly fuming. That Romano Vincenzo was her lover? Because he was certainly acting like one, she thought angrily, her aching head throbbing even more from the thought of being alone with him; from imagining the scene she didn't want, but which she knew would inevitably follow.

'Are you going to be all right?' the lingering Fran whispered protectively to her.

Libby darted a glance towards Luca's brother. His sheer physical presence and that dark charisma sent something like untapped electricity crackling across her nerve-endings.

'Of course,' she croaked, not at all sure she would be before Fran, too, went the same way as the others and the front door banged loudly behind them all.

An interminable silence filled the flat as Libby faced hard, unrelenting features across the carpeted space of her sitting room.

'What the devil did you think you were doing?' Her voice shook with her own hot emotion. 'What gave you the right to come in here and speak to my guests so rudely?' Hardly guests! she thought with a mental grimace, immensely relieved that he had driven them away, even if she didn't approve of the way he had done it.

'Forgive me if I broke up such a wildly enjoyable party.' The deep tones were anything but contrite. 'I would have thought even you would have had the decency to skip the good time when you've just been informed of how much your child needs you. Obviously it means far less to you than entertaining your precious friends!'

'They aren't my friends!'

His head cocked to one side. 'No?'

'Well, only one of them is and—'

'Evidently!'

Libby stifled a small, despairing sigh. It was clear he meant the man who had been forcing his attentions upon her.

'Steve Cullum was *drunk*,' she emphasised, as though that would somehow vindicate her. 'And they came here uninvited!'

'But it didn't take you long to get into the swing of things!'

Which is what it would have looked like, Libby realised, especially if he had heard Steve shouting to everyone that she wanted to dance, which he probably had!

'I was going to ring you,' she said.

'When? Tonight?' His eyes were steel-hard, his voice sounding blatantly unconvinced. 'Or tomorrow—after the hangover?'

Well, of course, he would think that, Libby despaired.

He looked like an avenging angel, from the flawless sheen on his coat to the striking force in his unrelenting features. There were raindrops glistening on his black hair, she noticed now, watching, mesmerized, as one fell from the thick strands to meet the startling contrast of his immaculately white collar.

She opened her mouth to speak, to assure him that not a drop of alcohol had passed her lips, but he cut across her protest, saying smoothly, 'You forget. I know you, Libby.' There was a cruel reminder in his softly spoken words. 'Perhaps even better than Luca did.'

'That's what you think,' she argued bitterly, and from the way his mouth pulled down one side knew exactly what he was remembering. Hadn't he stumbled upon her here in England, five months pregnant, supposedly caring for her father, but instead living it up with friends in his father's country club? He hadn't listened to her excuses then, so she didn't see any reason why he would listen to them now. 'What did you want anyway?' she asked wearily, turning her back on him.

He watched her clearing up glasses, stoop to pick up a cushion, toss it onto a chair.

He'd come back to apologise, he reflected with self-chastening mockery. To apologise for the way he had spoken to her today. It had been unwarranted, he'd decided afterwards, especially offering to pay her to accompany him back to Italy. Knowing the manager of the hotel where she was supposed to be tonight, he had tried to ring her there, and been relieved to learn that she hadn't attended the party after all. She had gone up a few notches in his estimation then and, as he'd made his way to her apartment, he'd been doubly ashamed of his behaviour, but his desire to make amends, he realised grimly now, had been far too premature!

The wide scoop-neck of her top had been pulled down on one side—probably by that inebriated lout who had been manhandling her, he thought—while her hair lay like a twist of fire against the pale silken slope of her shoulder. He felt a kick in his gut from watching the sway of her marginally curved hips as she went through into the kitchen, his eyes resting on her small, tight denim-clad bottom, his teeth clamping together from the host of temptations that he knew had once ensnared his brother.

'We parted on a rather unfortunate note,' he answered her from the kitchen doorway. 'It was my intention to rectify that.' After all, he could hardly persuade her to go back with him with threats and insults, he'd assured himself earlier, but that was before he had come up here, seen first-hand what little feeling this girl really had. 'In the circumstances,' he breathed, his anger with her spilling over from mere disillusionment into something hot and irrationally possessive, 'it seems all I have to apologise for is spoiling your fun!'

That it had even occurred to him to apologise for anything was unimaginable to Libby. The great Romano Vincenzo contrite? Even the thought of it was laughable.

A bitter little smile touched her mouth as, finding his proximity in the doorway of her small kitchen too unsettling, she couldn't think of anything to say.

She wanted to move away from him back into the larger room, but one darkly clad sleeve was stretched across the doorway, effectively blocking her way out.

Libby swallowed. 'C-could you let me pass, please?'

His eyes, probing into the wary depths of hers were far, far too disturbing. 'Of course.' She caught a waft of his cologne as he dropped his arm and she inhaled sharply, every nerve cell honing to his scent, his warmth, the closeness of his strong, hard body. But he didn't move and without looking at him she made to brush past him, stifling a small startled cry as his arm came up unexpectedly again, trapping her there against the doorjamb.

'Let me go!'

He laughed softly at her proud, indignant features. 'I wasn't aware that I was holding you.' His other hand came to rest disconcertingly just above her other shoulder.

Breath locking in her lungs, Libby darted a cautious glance up at him. Her heart was pumping as fast as if she had been running hard. 'You've got nothing to gain from this.'

She didn't know why she said it, every nerve tingling with apprehension and something far more complex as he turned her towards him, surveying her with a twist of cruel mockery on his lips.

'On the contrary,' he murmured, gazing down into her flushed and guarded features, 'I think I've got a great deal to gain.'

His thumb moved caressingly over the bared, heated flesh of her shoulder, his touch so light—just a whisper of sensation—that she might have been imagining it if it hadn't been for the way her breasts ached from her sick reaction to it, or for the shaming impulses that seemed to be causing implosions throughout her body, weakening her bones from a dark and shattering desire.

She wondered what it would be like to be pressed against his hard warmth, feel that devastating mouth—all that she could focus on now—clamped over hers; the startling realisation that he was drawing her towards him causing her mouth to part on a small gasp, her head to drop back in involuntary invitation to him so that his face went out of focus as he dipped his head and her wild and reckless craving became reality.

Sensation piled upon sensation as his mouth came down hard over hers, hostility meeting desire in one sizzling cauldron of hot, ungovernable expression.

He hadn't shaved since this morning and the angry graze of his jaw was a delicious friction against her soft skin as his mouth plundered hers with punishing thoroughness.

Libby groaned into his mouth, her mind despairing even as her body welcomed it, welcomed the arms that were suddenly tightening like steel bands around her, bringing her shockingly alive to the whipcord strength of him beneath his impeccable clothes and to the startling awareness of just how turned on he was.

Her errant, adolescent dreams about him, she realised, hadn't prepared her for this! Nor had she imagined she could know such…*wanting*…

With another small groan—induced only by desire now—she leaned into him, mind and body yielding together in some crazy sacrifice to an irrational need.

She hated him—and yet she wanted him!

Her limbs weakening with that acceptance, she clutched at his broad shoulders like someone clinging to a precipice, her red-tipped nails curling desperately against the dark, damp fabric of his raincoat.

Driven by her response, Romano felt his body hardening with an urge that made it almost hurt. It would be so easy to forget himself; to take her and all that her gloriously feminine body promised. He had wanted this girl for far longer than he cared to remember; wanted her so much she was the only woman who had ever made him disgusted with himself for entertaining such thoughts about her, especially while she was married to his brother. While he had had to bear it in silence, ignore the way her big doe eyes swept coyly away from him like some shy little virgin's whenever he spoke to her on some occasions, while on others they had seemed to challenge his with a sophistication well beyond her years!

But now there was no reason for restraint.

He jerked her against him, catching the small, stifled cry she uttered as though she was fighting her own battle between rejection and desire. But the thought of Luca and the mercenary way this girl had behaved was already cooling his ardour. Was he being extremely unwise even considering taking her back with him?

Confusion registered in her emerald eyes as he steeled himself to draw away from her. What was he thinking of? Could he not do without this added complication right now?

'Since it was your clear intention to wind up in someone's bed tonight,' he none the less felt compelled to taunt softly, 'perhaps you should make it mine? I can give you pleasure if that's what you're so hungry for, Libby. And I think I can guarantee you more satisfaction than you'd have found in the arms of that drunken lout who was here just now.'

Libby couldn't move—couldn't think—aware only of one long, tanned finger making light, sensuous circles over her bare shoulder and the tap, dribbling into the sink, that someone must have used and neglected to turn off properly.

All she could focus on was what Romano—her late husband's

brother and the man she despised—was suggesting, while her brain made unwilling comparisons with the man who had been there earlier. Romano Vincenzo wouldn't force himself on a woman the way Steve Cullum had. He wouldn't need to. He would be subtle, using his voice and his lips and hands with such articulated skill…

Reminding herself again of just who he was, head dropping back against the doorjamb, she was determined not to let him see how much his suggestion had fazed her. Heart pounding in her breast, her temples throbbing from her headache and her outlandish response to him, somehow she managed to query pointedly, 'Are you propositioning me?'

His smile was without warmth. 'And wind up in the same bittersweet trap as my brother?'

So he wasn't. He was only playing with her, she realised. Weighing her reactions—which had probably been behind the reason for that kiss—just to see how easily he could get his brother's scheming little widow into his bed! And she had fallen into his trap! Even if he had been more than a little out of control himself. Those black eyes still glinted with hot primal desire, yet behind it burned open hostility too.

With a surprising degree of force she pushed at the arm that was blocking the doorway and got herself out of his disturbing sphere, catching his soft laughter as she wrestled with the fact that even touching him like that gave her a whole host of unwelcome responses to deal with.

'We'll leave the day after tomorrow.'

His change of subject was so abrupt that it unbalanced her for a moment, shaken as she was from the shaming way she had responded in his arms.

'What?' Swinging to face him, she couldn't stop herself wondering what woman wouldn't fall victim to his dark attraction. Even now his stark masculinity was making her stomach muscles curl like brittle leaves.

'I gathered from that comment you made about ringing me that you have decided to heed my request and come back with me. Or am I being naïve in presuming that you've even allowed it any headroom with so much else going on in your life?'

An angry retort sprang to her lips, but wisely she bit it back. It would have been futile anyway, she told herself on a frustrated little sigh.

Wearily she said, 'Yes, I'm coming.'

'Good.' He strode away from her, turning in the doorway to assess her; her bright, dishevelled hair, the dark half-moons under her emotion-strained eyes and her cheeks, which she knew were flushed from more than just a pounding headache. 'Get a couple of good nights' sleep. I wouldn't want my nephew to see any remaining traces of the good-time girl in his mother.'

Tight-lipped, Libby swung away from him, her arms clutched tensely around herself to stem the urge to hit him rather than take any more of his jibes.

'And *cara*…' the endearment was so out of character at that moment and so sexily soft, she thought she was imagining it as she turned round with her arms still locked around her and met the cruel mockery on his lips. '…turn off that tap.'

CHAPTER THREE

'WHAT have you got in here?' Romano grimaced a couple of days later at the airport when he was hauling her suitcase out of the boot of the large chauffeur-driven saloon. 'Next spring's whole fashion collection?'

Libby dragged in a breath. Naturally he would think that, she thought waspishly, her tone brittle as she answered in the only way she knew he would expect her to. 'Bang on the nail!'

He sliced her a glance as he slammed the boot closed, hitting it twice to indicate to their driver that he could pull away. 'Thinking of partying while you're staying out there with us in Italy?'

'I could be,' she responded, keeping pace with his stride as he guided her towards the busy terminal. Nothing was further from her mind, however, and, deciding that she was carrying this charade a little too far, she added in defence of herself, 'Well, I wasn't quite sure what to bring or...how long I'd be staying.' A ton weight seemed to press down on her chest as she said that. 'I've also brought a few things for Giorgio.'

Like what? Romano thought. Things to soften him up to make up for the years she hadn't been around? What was she hoping to do? Buy her way into the kid's affections?

With features cast of stone he considered how easily she had given him up—as women like her could—without a backward glance, without a second thought as to how he would feel all the time he was growing up. Whether he was well. Being kindly treated. Happy.

As he held back for her to precede him through the automatic door into the terminal, he wondered if perhaps he was being too hard on his brother's widow. After all, she had agreed to come, which was more than he had expected, he conceded with a grim compression of his mouth, and she would naturally want to try to win Giorgio's trust in the only way she probably knew how.

The journey in the private jet was a far from relaxed one for Libby, sitting there uncomfortably aware of Luca's darkly brooding older brother in the seat opposite.

He had made small talk with her at first about inconsequential things, controlling the conversation, taking the lead. Then he spent the rest of the time working on his laptop on the narrow table in front of him, his ebony head bent, his mind anywhere but with Libby, who sat gazing at the rain streaming down the small round window beside her, listening to those deft, dark fingers moving with surprisingly alacrity over the keys.

'Do you want anything?' he asked when a pretty stewardess came and enquired if she could bring them some refreshment, glancing up at Libby in a way that made her stomach flip.

Only for these nerves to stop plaguing me! she prayed silently, shaking her head. She couldn't eat or drink. Not now. Not when she was only a couple of hours away from seeing her baby again.

'It might be some time before you get another chance.' Romano's expression held a surprising degree of concern. 'Are you sure?'

'Yes, I'm sure,' Libby replied tightly, but couldn't tell him that she was too knotted up inside to swallow a thing.

What would Giorgi look like? she wondered, fearful of being rejected. He wouldn't remember her, but would there be a bond there? A tug of something he'd recognise? Would he take to her? Or would she just be a total stranger walking into his life?

A cold, sick fear trickled through her as she considered the alternative. It would be his birthday in less than three weeks. Was he old enough yet to have begun to despise her for what she had done? And if he was, would he ever forgive her? Judge her less harshly if he knew how much she had wanted to see him? How hard she had tried—and how many times—only to be denied access on every occasion?

Once when she had been in Italy, modelling a new fashion collection, she'd read somewhere that the Vincenzos were there in Milan. She'd found out where they were staying and lingered outside the palatial hotel until she'd caught a glimpse of Luca's mother coming out of the main entrance, tugging the reluctant little two-year-old after her. She'd caught snatches of his baby chatter but had scarcely understood a word of it. He was a totally Italian child, lost to her even before the waiting limousine had swallowed him up and the vehicle sped away. It had taken her months to get over it. It had been like giving him up all over again.

'Here.' A plate of delicately prepared sandwiches was being thrust in front of her. In a half-daze, Libby took it, looking down at them. Smoked salmon and soft cheese, garnished with a twist of lemon and tomato. Tempting in other circumstances.

'I didn't…'

'I know.' A firm masculine hand insisted when she made to pass the unwanted meal back to him. *It will make you feel better*, his eyes, dark and sagacious, conveyed.

Had he guessed how she was feeling? Libby wondered. Was he aware of the turmoil going on inside of her? Of her fear and apprehension—her overriding guilt? If he was, then he was probably thinking that it was no more than she deserved, she thought chillingly, biting into one of the soft white sandwiches, if he really believed that she'd handed over her baby just because the price was right.

She was glad when the flight was over, though her nervousness only increased when another luxury saloon that had been waiting for them when they touched down brought them finally to the small hilltop castle where she had been so unhappy during her brief marriage. It was late in the afternoon and the sun struck gold from its crenellated roof, from its ancient ochre stone walls.

Memories crowded in around her as Romano ushered her through its familiar shaded courtyard with its lichen-clad fountain—surrounded now by tubs of bright geraniums—and into its imposing interior, their footsteps resounding intrusively across the great hall.

'I'm scared,' Libby admitted before she had realised it. Scared of those memories. Of the reception she might receive from a woman who had never failed to show her dislike of her. But most of all, of Giorgio's reaction to meeting her.

'Don't be,' Romano advised succinctly, and then, failing to understand entirely, 'He's just a kid who's trying to make sense of why his mother hasn't been around for the past six years. Now, let Angelica show you to your rooms,' he recommended as the elderly housekeeper, whom Libby remembered as the only friendly face other than Luca's, appeared to greet them. 'You'll find me in the drawing room when you're ready.'

Which didn't help, Libby thought, but said nothing. After all, there was no excuse for what she had done—as far as he was concerned. She was glad to leave him and take a few minutes to gather her composure as she followed the stooped and chatty little figure of Angelica up the stairs. She was even more relieved to discover that her suite of rooms—decorated in warm, natural hues against richly pattered soft furnishings—was in the opposite wing from the one she had occupied with Luca.

In fact, the place had had a considerable face-lift since she had walked out of here—alone and devastated after the loss of her husband and then the handing over of her baby—and quite recently if the smell of fresh paint, which she'd noticed as soon as she'd entered the house, was anything to go by. The place was generally brighter all round and less oppressive than it had been when both Romano's parents were alive. The odd extension had been added too, she noted, glancing out across the beautiful Italianate walled garden, which now boasted a pergola on the other side of the glittering blue oval of the pool. She had always loved the grounds, an oasis above the wooded valley. She remembered them being slightly more unkempt, but from the extent of new planting, abundant sculptures and unfamiliar, already established trees, she guessed that Romano had probably had a free hand for some time.

The only thing that looked the same was the drawing room. Or perhaps she failed to notice any changes, she would consider later, because all she was aware of when she entered was Romano Vincenzo, jacket and tie discarded, standing there alone beside the huge fireplace, looking every bit the lord of the manor amongst the familiar backdrop of original paintings, priceless antiques and rich tapestries.

Looking at a folded newspaper, he tossed it down on a side-table when he saw her come in.

Libby sent an anxious glance around her.

'Where is he?' Nerves, coupled with the effect he was having on her, made it sound almost like an accusation because she was trying not to fill her eyes with the whipcord power of his body, or that black hair, which fell tantalisingly over the back of his collar, mirroring that virile sprinkling of hair in the open 'V' of his shirt beneath the dark corded strength of his throat. 'Where's my son?'

An elevated eyebrow seemed to question her right even to use the term, but all he said in those deep calm tones of his was, 'Patience, *mia cara*. I have told them that you're here.'

Them? Of course, Libby reasoned, her head swimming with apprehension. Sophia Vincenzo was still very much in residence here.

Her stomach muscles tightened, making her feel almost sick, and suddenly, as her gaze strayed reluctantly over Romano's long, lean body, all the years fell away and she was that overawed eighteen-year-old bride again, afraid of making a bad impression, hoping against hope for the acceptance that had never come.

Then she had had Luca's protection, she remembered, and instantly ridiculed herself for using such a dramatic word. What did she need protection from? She was here only because of Giorgio—because her little boy needed her. Yet her mind refused to discard the memory of that kiss in her apartment two nights ago, the sensations that had shamed her still leaping into life in the tingling of her breasts and the deep throb in her lower body whenever she thought about them.

'What are you thinking?' Romano asked, and there was menace in his slow stride as he approached her with that same intimidating aura of self-assured arrogance, that pulsing sexuality that brought goosepimples out on her flesh. 'Are you thinking what I am? That in all this there's a remarkable sense of *déjà vu*?'

Libby's tongue seemed to cleave to the roof of her mouth. 'No,' she lied, because even the way he was looking at her was making her feel as stripped and exposed as it had done seven years ago. 'Things are different now, Romano,' she reminded him, drawing herself up to her full, remarkable height in her staunch determination that they would be.

'Indeed they are,' he whispered, those glittering eyes appraising her figure beneath the white sleeveless T-shirt and soft blue trousers she had worn on the plane with a mocking sensuality that made her senses quiver. His voice, though, held only contempt, each word cruelly barbed as he tagged on, 'Now you no longer have the...*inconvenience* of a wedding ring.'

Eyes darting to his, Libby made to deliver an angry retort, her heart pounding from the speculation of exactly what he had meant by that. But the door opened at that moment and Sophia Vincenzo came in, older and yet as graceful still as Libby remembered her with her elegant clothes and her beautifully coiffured greying hair, but it was to the little boy with the impish black eyes—Luca's eyes—under a mop of unruly brown hair that Libby's urgent gaze flew.

Giorgi!

'Zio!' Those eyes lighting up, the boy would have run towards his uncle if Sophia hadn't stopped him. A restraining hand on his young shoulder, she was stooping to issue a low instruction in her own language.

'How do you do?' Giorgio said to Libby in a small, stilted voice, his formality—his accent—so much a part of these people that something seemed to wrench the connective tissues of her heart.

Dropping down to his level, she wanted to reach out and clasp him to her. Bury her lips in the soft sable of his hair and sob out how much she had missed him—loved him! How every minute that she had been parted from him had been a private hell. But she didn't want to do anything that would make Giorgio withdraw from her; alienate him before she had even stepped onto the first rung on this very fragile ladder. Besides, Sophia Vincenzo's gnarled fingers were planted possessively on each little shoulder. Like an eagle's talons, Libby thought distractedly. An eagle refusing to relinquish a prized and coveted little lamb.

'I'm very well,' she restrained herself by saying in a voice she couldn't keep from trembling as, uncomfortably aware of Romano standing above her now, she took the small hand that was being offered. 'And you?'

The little boy stared at her for a moment before tilting his head right back to glance up at his grandmother.

'Nonna told me to say that,' he confessed somewhat sheepishly, before sending a rather troubled look towards his uncle.

Libby saw a surprisingly gentle smile touch Romano's mouth. He said something softly to the boy in Italian, which she roughly interpreted from the classes she had forced herself to take in the eternal hope of seeing her son again one day as encouragement for Giorgio to say whatever he felt comfortable saying.

The little boy's forehead puckered as he turned to Libby again and asked after a few moments, 'Are you really my mamma?' At Romano's prompting he was much more relaxed, all formality and artifice gone.

'Yes, Georgio.' Achingly dry-mouthed, Libby held her breath, wondering where that admission on her part was going to lead.

Surveying her with a far more sombre expression, his young head tilted to one side, seriously he enquired, 'Are you going to be here for my birthday?'

Libby gave a tremulous little laugh—not expecting that at all—and heard Romano chuckle; his mother's terse response, correcting her grandson.

Of course, she thought, smiling through the tears she was fighting to keep under control. Such things were vastly important to a child.

'You bet!' she breathed, her hand softly shaping his face, not caring what Romano or his mother thought. She wasn't going to miss another of his birthdays if they tried to drag her out of this house screaming.

Giorgio gave her a semi-toothless smile where already his second teeth were pushing through, little pointers that even now were marking the road towards manhood. Reality chilled her, causing every cell to ache with the knowledge of just how much of his little life she had already missed.

'Oh, *buono*! Zio Romano says he's going to buy me a new bicycle. I wanted a bigger one, but Zio says I can't have one of those until I'm a year older. Zio says he will teach me to ride it when the time comes!'

And clearly Zio Romano was the be-all and end-all! Libby decided resentfully. 'You speak very good English,' she uttered to Giorgio, nevertheless amazed.

'My son has always insisted his nephew acknowledge both sides of his heritage,' Sophia supplied in that same chilling tone for which Libby had always remembered her, although as those familiar golden eyes raked over her Libby suspected that Sophia Vincenzo wasn't entirely in agreement with Romano's decision.

'I speak Italian as well!' Suddenly a little hand was reaching out to touch the fiery swathe that fell like burnished silk across Libby's shoulder. Rather more coyly the little boy said, 'I *like* your hair.'

Something clutched at Libby's heart, squeezing it until she thought the blood was being sapped from her veins, while behind them a deep voice drawled, 'Beware of such things. They'll be your downfall, Georgio.'

The little boy frowned again, not understanding, but the censure behind Romano's remark didn't fail to connect with Libby.

He thought she was a gold-digger, only marrying his brother for what she could get out of him—just as his parents had, she reminded herself bitterly. So naturally he would want to warn his nephew against women like her!

'I like yours too,' she breathed, ruffling its soft brown mass and noticing how the light from the long windows picked out the red highlights, a legacy she had passed on to him—part of her own genes—no matter how many years had separated them, how many miles.

'Would you like to see my bedroom?' Giorgio invited with a little conspiratorial smile.

Five years old! Libby thought, and already he had coquetry off to a fine art! Yet he reminded her so much of Luca trying to placate her for coming in later than promised after a night out with friends—and he'd had so many friends because he'd been so easy-going—that a poignant emotion stabbed her, bitter-sweet, cuttingly deep.

'I'd like that very much,' she breathed, her mouth trembling.

As the little boy took her hand to lead her off, out of the corner of her eye she caught the swift gesture Romano made, restraining his mother.

So he realised she needed time alone with her child, Libby recognised, begrudging him the small dart of gratitude she owed him for that.

The suite of rooms that was obviously the nursery contained everything she would expect to find in a child's personal play area. Posters of famous fictional characters. A computer. Games and puzzles. And, sitting on a chest, propped up against the far wall of this typical little boy's room, a golden teddy with one ear missing, its mock fur worn away from nearly six years of being loved to death.

Libby moved over and picked it up.

'That's Caesaro,' Giorgio informed her importantly. 'I had him when I was little. Nonna says I'm too old for him now, but Zio said I shouldn't let him go just because he's old and can't hear very well any more. This is my *mamma,* Caesaro.' He reached up and, with his hand sheilding his mouth, gabbled something in the bear's single ear. 'He says he can't speak either,' he told Libby, grinning. 'That is why he hasn't said *buon giorno* to you.'

Looking down at the furless little bear, emotion clogging her throat, somehow Libby managed to whisper, 'We've already met.'

She had bought the teddy for Giorgio when he was ten days old and it had gone with him the day she had handed him over. The day her life had ended. She couldn't bear to think about that.

'Why are you crying?' The little boy was looking at her with those huge, dark, impish eyes that were so like his father's. 'Are you unhappy?'

'No, Giorgi.' What could she say to him? There was so much she needed to say, and yet she couldn't find the words.

Dropping down to her knees, suddenly all she could do was clutch him to her, holding him close, her hand cradling his soft head while scalding tears squeezed out from beneath her tightly closed eyelids.

'Why did you go away?'

Pain constricted her throat. How could she answer that? How could she begin to explain to this innocent little boy—her own child—the circumstances that had forced her into giving him up? She couldn't do it. Not without incriminating the people he loved. The only family he had grown up with.

Sniffing back tears, she straightened, brushing his hair back with a loving hand. She had to tell him something. But what?

'She went away because she had to,' a deep masculine voice intoned from the doorway. 'Because she's a very busy lady.'

Romano strode in. A dominating figure. Cool. Self-possessed. Totally relaxed.

Libby met his eyes, not warm and mischievous like Luca's but shrewd and penetrating, glitteringly black. All she could manage was a flicker of a smile as she got to her feet.

She couldn't tell him how grateful she was that his timely intervention—however discriminatingly slanted towards her—had rescued her from having to answer such a difficult question, because it seemed to satisfy the little boy.

'Are you busy now?' Giorgio enquired, his spirits seeming to drop a little.

'No. No, I've got all the time you want, Giorgi,' she assured him softly, because the shoots and commitments, her agent and her manager and anyone else who thought they were more important than bonding with her son could wait.

'And you're not going away again, are you?'

What could she say? *No. I'll never go away again! I'll never leave you like I did before!*

She looked desperately to Romano to rescue her for a second time. It wasn't up to her, was it? He wasn't helping her this time, however, and, though she'd already decided she would move heaven and earth to keep her son with her this time, she knew that whatever Romano Vincenzo decided would be law. He was the child's legal guardian now after all.

'Let's take each day as it comes, Giorgio,' she advised gently, just as a maid came in to tell them that Signora Vincenzo was insisting that they join her for tea.

Libby noticed the way Romano's mouth seemed to tighten.

'Why don't you run along and tell your grandmother we will be down shortly?' he suggested to his nephew, adding something in Italian that Libby didn't catch when he sensed an obvious reluctance that made the little boy whoop with joy.

'What did you say to him?' Libby asked as soon as they were alone again.

'I find a pay-off usually works no matter how young or how innocent the recipient,' Romano returned drily, reminding her all too acutely of the pay-off she had received from his father on handing over her baby—as he had intended to. The brush of his hand against hers as he relieved her of the teddy she had forgotten she was still holding made her catch her breath. 'I promised he could stay up an hour later tonight.'

And he would rest assured in the knowledge that his Uncle Romano would keep his promises, Libby thought, under no misconception of how much her son loved and respected Luca's elder brother. As he should have loved and trusted her…

'I've missed so much of his life. I don't recognise him any more,' she uttered, despairing at the years that had flown and could never be replaced. 'I don't know him.'

'It's hardly surprising, is it?' he said, dispensing with the little bear on the pillow above the bright red racing car that patterned the coverlet on the little single bed. *When you relinquished all claim to him when he was two months old!*

Straightening, he had to bite his tongue to stop himself from saying it, and saw her almost visibly flinch as though his unspoken thoughts had had the power to flay her.

He had to confess, though, that that show of emotion just now when he had come in and caught her sobbing had surprised him. Downstairs she had seemed far too restrained, almost unaffected, for a mother reunited with her son after so long. Yet reluctantly now he found himself questioning just how deep her feelings might go; if she was actually capable of experiencing real maternal love.

Memories, long buried and denied, rose like spectres out of the ashes of his own childhood, but mentally he shook them aside. Coming back to the present, he forced himself to acknowledge that guilt too could produce tears like those he had witnessed just now—and this girl had a lot to feel guilty over. Beautiful, with a heaven-sent face and figure—and mercenary beyond belief! *Santo cielo*! He admonished himself for even wanting to be taken in.

Soften towards her and he would be the same kind of manipulated fool that Luca had been!

'Well, congratulations!' he found himself grinding out tersely, even while he knew it would do nothing to help the tense relations that already existed between them. 'I'm sure you managed to convince him of your good intentions with that remarkably touching performance.'

Libby almost staggered under the sting of his lashing censure. Was that what he thought this was? she wondered, agonised. A performance?

'Yes, well…I could hardly tell him the truth, now, could I?' she retorted acridly, refusing to let him see how much his condemnation of her hurt. 'That I was far too busy to bother with him before this.' Emphatically she twisted his earlier explanation around to express the meaning he had really intended to convey. 'And that keeping him would have messed up my life far too much!'

She would have pushed past him then if a strong hand hadn't reached out and caught her. His fingers bit into her arm as his glittering eyes searched hers, challenging and hard.

'Nor will you ever let him think that! Either now or at any time in the future!'

'Why not?' Forcibly she tugged out of his grasp. 'You think it!'

'That's different,' he assured her coldly. 'I'm made of…what is the phrase you use? Sterner stuff. And I know how to handle beautiful, heartless little social climbers like you.'

She wanted to fling at him that he couldn't handle a dinner party. That he was such a prejudiced oaf he wouldn't recognise honesty if he spooned it out of his soup!

Instead, with forced composure and a twisted little smile that she knew would do her no favours, she said, 'Do you, Romano? I wonder,' and then feared from the dark emotion that leaped in those beautiful eyes that she had provoked him just that bit too far.

As both hands locked onto her shoulders, she saw the determined purpose in his eyes and, every nerve racing with a dangerous excitement, Libby steeled herself for the humiliation she knew would come.

'We're both single-minded.' His voice was menacingly low, his long black lashes lowered as his gaze rested on the trembling fullness of her mouth. 'We both go after exactly what we want.'

'Do we?' Was that her voice? So faint? So croaky? 'Don't bracket me with yourself,' somehow she managed to get out, while her heart seemed to be pumping so fast she thought it would burst, 'or with any other member of your wonderful family, *please*!'

He laughed low in his throat. 'You did that yourself when you made the very foolish mistake of marrying my brother.'

'Not foolish, Romano. I had everything I wanted.' Which was Luca's love! she thought wildly and with a fervour that left no room for any doubt. And Giorgio! All the pain she suffered throughout her marriage and since had been worth it to know that there was Giorgio.

'Did you?'

His stripping regard caused her brows to come together. What was he doing? Trying to cast doubt on the one thing about her life here that had been any good?

'If you're referring to Vincenzo finances then yes, I can imagine that you would have felt as though you'd landed in a bed of roses. But if you're talking about anything else…' a mocking sensuality curved that devastatingly masculine mouth '…then I think it would have taken very little on my part to show Luca exactly what a fickle little creature you were when it boiled down to loyalty.'

Libby swallowed. What was he saying? That her failure to be cowed by his rampant superiority sometimes had been some sort of come-on?

You scared the hell out of me! she wanted to scream, but her lips wouldn't seem to move.

'As I said, *mia cara*, we both know what we want. And exactly how to get it.'

Libby's eyes darted anxiously to his. After her shaming—if inexplicable—response to him in her flat the other day, he couldn't fail to have realised how profoundly he affected her. Even if he thought she'd been nursing some ungovernable desire to leap into bed with him when she had been married to his brother! But would he really spell it out? Show her? Not in Giorgio's room surely! she thought hectically. And maybe he was thinking along the same lines because suddenly he released her and, with remarkable control and a courteous sweep of his arm that seemed ludicrous in the circumstances, he breathed, '*Allora*? Shall we go down?'

CHAPTER FOUR

LIBBY spent the next day getting to know her son. He was remarkably bright for his age, she discovered, watching how capable he was on his computer, and she was amazed by how well he could already read and write.

'That used to be one of my favourites too,' she told him fondly when he showed her his best-loved story book, remembering the characters that her father had brought to life so vividly for her before she had been old enough to read about them for herself.

If only life could have been more simple! If only he hadn't been so ill. If only Luca hadn't died! How different things would have been, she thought achingly.

'Zio said he's going to take me out with him today and that you can come too,' Giorgio informed her importantly when he was returning the book to his brightly painted little bookcase. 'You will come, won't you, Mamma?' he implored.

How she had longed for and dreaded that she might never hear her son call her that! 'You try and stop me!' she laughed, ruffling his hair.

With mixed emotions, though, Libby licked suddenly dry lips. Just why did this longed-for reunion have to come with such a price? Have to include Romano Vincenzo when she despised the man; when she was so drawn to him physically that she despised herself for it in equal measure?

'He's very good to you…your Uncle Romano, isn't he?' she ventured, reluctantly fishing for any snippet of information she could get about Luca's brother. It was surprising, she thought, that, though he had left such a mark on her past, and she was well aware of the power he wielded both in and outside the family circle, she knew remarkably little about the real man, what it was that made this deep, dark billionaire tick.

'Oh, *si!*' Giorgio confirmed enthusiastically. 'And when I grow up I'm going to be just like him.'

'Perhaps your mother has other opinions about that.'

Heart leaping from the deep voice that sliced across the silence, Libby swung round, her bright hair swishing like silk against her tight tense shoulders.

Wearing black jeans that hugged his powerful hips and a casual yet superbly tailored ivory shirt, Romano Vincenzo looked all that he was: hard, lean and so powerfully sexy that Libby's blood seemed to fizz in response.

'Perhaps she has,' she couldn't help lobbing back in defence against all she was feeling.

His smile seemed to mock the unmistakable wobble in her voice.

'I'm driving into town,' he said. 'Perhaps Giorgio's mentioned we'd deem it a pleasure if you came with us.'

'Well…he didn't put it that nobly,' she remarked with a sceptical lift of her brows, aware that for Romano certainly her presence would be anything but a pleasure.

'I'll be leaving in twenty minutes,' he stated, clearly refusing to be drawn into any altercation with her and taking her acceptance for granted as he turned away.

It was a surprisingly enjoyable day. Romano took them to one of the small neighbouring towns and Libby waited with Giorgio in the large 4 x 4 while he settled some business in the bank.

She was showing Giorgio some photographs she had brought with her when Romano rejoined them. Snaps of Luca and herself together. Her own mother holding her as a baby, and her likeness to Giorgio struck her so fiercely that it took her breath away.

'And that's your English grandfather. *Nonno*,' she translated, emotion pressing on her chest as a little hand took the snapshot of the man leaning on his spade in the cottage garden he had loved, and which she always carried in her purse.

'Your father?' From the driver's seat, Romano glanced over his shoulder at the photograph Giorgio was studying.

She nodded.

'Where is he now?'

'He died.' She didn't want to share the knowledge with him, for reasons, she thought bitterly, he would know only too well. 'Just over a year ago.'

'I'm sorry.'

Was he?

Surprisingly his eyes commiserated, but she didn't want his sympathy, either real or affected.

'Let's go, then, shall we?' she said, a little too brightly, as she slipped the retrieved photograph back into her purse, feeling those shrewd masculine eyes raking over her face before Romano pushed the car into gear and pulled away.

After that things became a little more relaxed for a while when Romano took them both to lunch in a friendly-run café where the waiters made a great fuss of Giorgio and presented him with a red balloon on a string, which he promptly popped so that they had to go and find him another, and they all came out laughing. High-spirited. Relaxed. Like a family, Libby found herself thinking, and killed that ridiculous notion the second it was born.

Despite his opinion of her, however, Romano kept the conversation amiable. Obviously for the benefit of his nephew, Libby decided caustically, yet grateful for it as they wandered into a shop to help Giorgio select new trainers.

'I want to buy them for him,' Libby expressed, when he had chosen the pair he wanted.

'That isn't necessary,' Romano drawled.

'Nevertheless, I'm going to,' she asserted, squatting down to help her son tie his laces before Romano could.

She caught the barest movement of a broad shoulder as she glanced up.

What was he thinking? she wondered as those darkly penetrating eyes regarding her from their vantage point caused that insidious tension to coil deep down in her loins. That it would take much more than that to make up for all the years she hadn't been around?

Her spirits were lowered as they made their way back to the car.

About to cross the relatively busy road, Romano caught Giorgio's hand. Automatically, the little boy's other hand came up to clasp his mother's.

Above his head, Libby's eyes connected involuntarily with Romano's. The innocent gesture on Giorgio's part seemed to link them together in a way she would rather have avoided and it was obvious her son was thinking along the same lines when, after tilting his head to look at first one and then the other, he enquired mortifyingly of her, 'Are you going to stay here forever and live with Zio and me?'

All Libby felt like doing was sinking into the concrete as they stepped onto the pavement on the other side of the road. How could she answer that? she wondered chaotically.

'I certainly won't be imposing on your…uncle…any longer than I have to,' she stated emphatically. The last thing she wanted to do was *live* with Romano Vincenzo!

'What does imposing mean?' Giorgio queried guilelessly, frowning up at them both in turn.

'Something to do with being where someone else doesn't want them to be,' Romano explained tightly. A moment later, passing an ice-cream vendor, he extracted a coin from the pocket of his jeans and, with a few words of Italian to Giorgio that rippled like silk off his tongue, sent his nephew racing off to claim his unexpected treat.

'Don't do that,' he ground out stiffly to Libby when the boy was out of earshot.

'Do what?' The soft anger in his voice had made her look up at him, bemused.

'Use the boy's innocence to air your obvious animosity towards me,' he stated through suddenly clenched teeth.

'I wasn't doing that,' she argued in defence, ashamed to realise that that was just what she had been in danger of doing. 'At least, that wasn't my intention.'

'Perhaps not,' he accepted, though his proud features were still inexorably set. 'I don't care how inconvenient or how uncomfortable this whole exercise might be for you, if you care for your son's welfare you will stay here as long as it is necessary, is that understood?'

There was no point telling him that she intended to. That she would be doing everything in her power to keep her son in her life now that she had found him again and that there was no way that he would be able to just cast her aside like an old sheet when he decided the time was right as easily as he was obviously hoping to do.

'I'm staying here because I want to, and not because of your or anyone's else's bullying tactics,' she returned with soft determination, pushing ahead of him then to follow Giorgio up to the ice-cream vendor.

Longing for a bath that evening to ease away the tensions of the day, Libby recoiled on finding the luxurious tub already taken by a startlingly large eight-legged occupant.

After she'd made several failed attempts at removing it herself and finally conceded that she would have to ring for assistance, her heart sank and then jerked into a violent rhythm when she answered the knock on her door and found Romano standing there.

'Angelica had a call about a large spider needing evicting from these quarters.' He was holding a wide-rimmed jar and appeared rather too smug for Libby's liking. She couldn't help noticing, though, that his hair was curling damply against his collar from where he had recently taken a shower, and that the fresh black and grey striped shirt he had teamed with dark, well-fitting trousers emphasised a masculinity that sent her traitorous hormones rocketing.

'I can do it myself,' she protested shakily when he strode casually in, uninvited. 'I only rang down for something wide enough to cover it with so I wouldn't risk damaging its legs.'

He gave her a look that doubted her capacity for feeling for any creature but herself, unsettling her further with his swift but penetrating appraisal of her short cotton robe, all she had on over her briefs.

'It's no trouble,' he drawled. 'I was coming up here anyway. I thought that if you find yourself with nothing to do, you might like to look at these.'

She glanced disparagingly at whatever it was he was dropping onto the dressing table.

Video cassettes?

Didn't he think her bright enough for the shelves of assorted reading she'd already browsed through when she'd come up here last night? What did he imagine would amuse her shallow mind? she thought tartly, uncomfortably conscious of those dark eyes still regarding her. Soaps? Some grisly horror movies? Or did they include a *Guide to Parenting* he'd picked up somewhere?

'Thanks,' she uttered without looking at him, and heard him moving away into the bathroom.

She looked flustered, Romano thought as he came back from consigning her other uninvited guest to the ivy outside the bathroom window. She was having trouble with the top drawer of the chest, which appeared to be stuck.

'Here. Let me,' he volunteered.

'I'm quite capable of doing a simple thing like closing a drawer!' she returned with an ungraciousness that instantly shamed her, but his nearness was causing a prickly sensation all over her skin and, besides, she had some very personal things in that drawer apart from her underwear!

'You have something caught here…' He pulled the drawer open wider, his investigative masculine fingers dark against the wisps of feminine-fine silks and lace. 'I think we've got it…'

He pulled it out carefully. It was a birthday card—obviously for Giorgio. An age card, fortunately undamaged.

He frowned down at it, an emotion he couldn't contain making him remark, 'The boy's six next birthday. Not five.' *Mamma mia!* Surely she wasn't so uncaring a mother that she had forgotten the age of her own child!

'Give me that!' Her reaction as she tried to snatch it from him surprised him. He pulled it out of her reach, the crease between his eyes deepening as he noticed that there were others stored to one side of the drawer.

'What do you think you're doing?' Libby's hand came up to try to stop him as he started rifling through them. 'You've no right!'

There was a card, he realised, for every year of his nephew's life.

He took out the one headed *Baby's First Christmas*; badly buckled, he noticed, and knew instinctively that it had been in that state before it had ever reached the drawer.

'Give that back to me!'

Driven on by something stronger than curiosity, he ignored her protests, feeling like an eavesdropper when he scanned the few heartfelt words she had written inside.

He dropped it back into the drawer, though not before noticing the photograph album with its gold lettering that spelt out *Our Baby's First Year*; more photographs of her parents and Luca. Small mementoes, worth nothing in themselves, but probably priceless to their owner.

Chillingly now he recalled his disparaging remarks about the contents of her case at the airport the previous day. Remembered what she had said in reply.

'I've...brought a few things for Giorgio.'

He remembered his derogatory thoughts in response to that remark and was ashamed of himself now for thinking what he had. She wasn't trying to buy herself into the boy's affections at all. This was a collection a loving mother would have kept. Which didn't quite match up with the mercenary creature he had always believed her to be.

'What's all this about?' he demanded, with a toss of his chin towards the items she obviously hadn't intended him to see.

'I don't have to explain myself to you!'

He slammed the drawer closed as she pivoted away from him, but his other arm shot out, catching her in mid-flight.

'I'm trying to understand!'

Her head came up and he saw a small vein pulsing in the hollow of her pale throat. 'Please! Don't strain yourself!'

'Libby!'

Her eyes were bright pools, glittering with anger and something else. What was it? he reasoned, his dark gaze probing mercilessly into their crystalline depths. Pain? Fear? Or just a denial of this raging desire that made his head spin from just touching her—just from breathing in her perfume, which was working like an aphrodisiac on his senses and doing untold things to his anatomy—and that ravaged her as surely as it ravaged him?

'You gave him up.' He had her by both elbows, felt like shaking an explanation out of her. Or was it the frustrations of his own past that he wanted to punish her for? 'You didn't want to be in his life!'

'So you keep reminding me!'

'I don't like having to spell this out, but it *was* your decision.'

Was it?

She didn't say it aloud. Just stood there staring accusingly at him with her face contorted in anguish. Did he really not know? Hadn't he been in on the conspiracy to hurt her in the most effective way possible if she'd refused to play ball and hand over her baby as his family had been demanding?

'Is that the reason for all *that?*' He jerked his head towards the chest and the sad little story of raw sentiment it contained. 'Guilt? Self-reproach? Regret?'

'If you're so certain of that—why ask?' she threw at him vehemently, because she had suffered all those things; because she should have found a way—been strong enough to fight them all. Her fears and insecurities. Luca's parents. *Him!*

Without her realising it her gaze had strayed to his mouth. That hard male mouth that had the power to slate her at every opportunity; that promised retribution, punishment, justice—and at the same time—heaven!

'Si, Libby.' His voice was a low, sensuous murmur. 'I want to understand that too.'

As he drew her closer, warning bells clamoured loudly across her instincts of survival, shrilling through a rising excitement that left her breathless and tense.

'Why every time I come near you, you give off signals that any man would be hard-pushed not to recognise. You always did.'

'You're imagining things! I was happily married to Luca!'

'Maybe. And maybe I was,' he intoned, 'but I'm certainly not imagining them now.'

Breasts lifting sharply, she stood, stock-still, in the circle of his arms, unable to think—to breathe.

'You want me, as much as I want you—except that I don't deny it. Tell me that you don't want me. Tell me that you haven't thought about this since the moment I kissed you or at any other time before that.'

She wanted to! But how could she, she despaired, when her body wanted to acknowledge it with an instinct as old as time? When she could feel the hardening peaks of her breasts pushing against the fine cotton of her robe, feel the heat building in that most feminine part of her that made her ache for him as she had never ached for any man?

'No.'

He laughed very softly, and lightly parted the edges of her

robe, slipping one off her shoulder before stooping to press his lips to the trembling flesh he had exposed.

Libby sucked in her breath, groaning, her eyes closing in denial because he had lifted his head to look at her and she couldn't bear to let him see the hunger that darkened her eyes, watch the slow curl of his devastating mouth as he acknowledged that he was right.

'No?' It was a low, teasing chuckle against her lips. She could feel the warmth of his breath mingling with hers, an erotic magnet willing her mouth to open and take the exquisite torture of his.

She tilted her head back, silently begging for his kiss now with a desperation that left her weak. But fulfilment wasn't on his agenda, she realised helplessly, when he brought his mouth to within a hair's breadth of hers time and again, only to withdraw every time he looked like granting her the consummation she craved.

Unreservedly, not caring any more what he thought, she reached up and dragged his head down to hers, her murmur a shameless plea against his lips.

He gave a low groan like a man unable to resist defeat, and Libby gasped sharply as he pulled her hard into him.

His arousal was obvious—as obvious as hers was secretive: just a slick trickle of heat she could feel moistening her panties, a silent preparation for a penetration that made her lower body contract hotly against the fine silk.

His hand was inside her robe, his warm palm such an erotic sensation against her breast that it made her cry out, giving her no room to think, to breathe.

He *wanted* her! She didn't know why it made her feel so powerful to know that—only that it did.

Feverishly she tugged at his shirt, catching his moan of pleasure as her hands ran over the fevered heat of his body, felt the flexing muscles of steel beneath velvet flesh.

She wanted *him!* And she didn't care how much he despised her. How sick was that? She didn't want to think about it as their tongues blended, mouths devouring in a mutually ungovernable act of savage need.

She was driving him crazy, Romano thought, unable to believe things had come this far since he had entered the room.

Drugged by her perfume, he let his mouth and hands burn across her eager body, her murmurs of wanting like sensuous nymphs dragging him down into a fire of need he wanted to be consumed by. The truth was he had never met such wild wanting in any woman—or known it in himself—until now.

Had she been the same with Luca? Shown him the heaven she was promising *him* now? Was he privileged to have produced such an uncontrolled response in her? Or was she just so deprived of sexual adventure at the moment that any man would have done?

He couldn't believe that, and yet the sudden memories of his brother chilled his ardour. For all her apparent concern for Giorgio, it still didn't alter the way she had treated Luca, marrying him for money then exchanging his child for a pay-off, no matter how much she denied it—or might have regretted it since.

'What is it?' she breathed, puzzled as he drew away.

'I came up here to rescue a spider. Now I'm rescuing myself,' he said coldly—much too coldly, he realised, but he couldn't help himself.

'What's that supposed to mean?' She was pulling her robe around her, breathing heavily, her expression a blend of wounded bewilderment and frustration. 'Was your only intention to see if you could get me into bed? Was that why you came up here instead of sending one of the maids up? To try and make a fool of me…?' Her voice tailed off on a sob. Under the magnanimous pretext of bringing up some videos!

'Libby…' He made a move towards her, but was stalled by Sophia Vincenzo's voice along the galleried landing.

They had both forgotten in their hunger, Libby realised, mortified, that the bedroom door was open!

She saw Romano stiffen, sensed the irritation in him at the untimely intervention.

'Oh, there you are, Romano!' Her elegant figure framed by the doorway, Sophia raked her golden eyes over Libby's dishevelled state before they took in Romano, who was casually retrieving an empty jar from the top of the chest.

Libby felt herself blushing hotly, guessing what the woman must think, although Romano, his shirt already tucked back into his waistband, seemed totally unperturbed by the situation.

'Yes, what is it?' he urged.

A subtle feminine glance strayed to Libby again. 'You're wanted on the phone.'

'All right! I'll be there now,' he told his mother with dismissive impatience, so that the woman retreated with a cool 'goodnight' to Libby.

Libby felt Romano's hand on her arm as she made to brush past him, her features flushed from the shame of what she had nearly let him do and then the embarrassment of virtually being discovered.

'For what it's worth, I didn't intend this to happen—not like this.'

He was massaging the back of his neck, and there were weary lines around his eyes, Libby noticed now, but couldn't help retaliating with, 'Really? How did you intend it to happen?'

With music and champagne after a romantic dinner, he surprised himself by thinking, but couldn't say it, knowing how cynical it would sound. He wasn't even sure he wasn't just being cynical himself. He knew what she was like. Hadn't he been born to be the victim of heartless women?

'It's been a traumatic couple of days. For all of us,' he added, releasing her. 'I'll leave you with those.' He indicated the cassettes he'd brought up as he turned to go. 'In the meantime, get a good night's rest.'

'Thanks!' Libby breathed after he had closed the door behind him, still shamed by what had happened and by the way he had brought those kisses to an abrupt halt. 'I'm sure they'll keep me suitably amused if I can't sleep!'

It was some time later, after she had taken her bath, that she went over to brush her hair and took a grudging look at the cassettes he had condescended to leave her.

Reading the label on the sleeve of the first one, she snatched it up, her fingers tensing as she reached for the second, then the third. These weren't cinema films or television documentaries!

Racing over to the television set, she switched it on, her hands trembling as she thrust the first cassette into the video recorder. They were simply home movies, all clearly marked with exactly what they contained.

In her simple cotton nightdress, with her damp hair curling wildly around her shoulders, she sat, devouring every image, sobbing and laughing in turn as precious moments of Giorgio's infancy unwound themselves before her eyes.

Giorgio tugging paper off his first Christmas presents. Giorgio taking his first steps. Now here he was riding his first pony with Romano instructing him on how to sit. In yet another clip he was sitting at the wheel of his uncle's red sports car, pretending to steer it, his young face alive with laughter and delight and such obvious awe of the man who was filming him that Libby felt a swift hard kick of painful envy.

He loved Romano! And why shouldn't he? she reasoned in an attempt to ease her blistering pain because the Vincenzos had had the boy's love and trust all the time he had been growing up, while she hadn't experienced a gram of it. After all, Romano had always been there for Giorgio—from the very beginning.

The night she had given birth to him had been a long and arduous one and she had had to bear it alone. Waiting. Hoping. Longing. Praying for Luca.

Unable to reach him on his cellphone, she had eventually been forced to telephone his mother, but when the pain of her long labour was over he still hadn't come or even called.

She remembered the moment of sheer joy and relief when a nurse had popped her head around the door and announced brightly, 'All's well, Mrs Vincenzo. Your husband's here.'

Disappointment and a sudden kicking-in of adrenalin caused her already plummeting hormones to plunge her into emotional chaos when it was Romano who strode in instead of Luca.

'Wh-What are you doing here?' Her voice faltered under the weight of her unease and that inexplicable tension that made her pulses throb at her temples.

'You've just brought the next generation of Vincenzos into the world,' he said, looking particularly virile in a black leather jacket thrown loosely over a white shirt and black trousers. 'I thought that at least one member of this family should acknowledge that.'

Shocked and unsettled by his arrival, and too disappointed to thank him for taking the trouble, she croaked weakly, 'Where's Luca?'

Looking up at him from her mountain of pillows she'd thought how weary he looked. There were creases around his eyes and a darker than usual shading around his mouth and jaw that somehow only added to the impression of hard masculinity. But it was as though he had flown there straight from one of his long European trips and hadn't yet had time to freshen up, she thought. Or as though he'd been scouring the Amazon for something! But then he answered. 'Luca...couldn't get away.' There was something uncharacteristically hesitant in the way he said it.

Disbelief seemed to contort not just her face so much as her whole body.

'Why not?' she wailed, ready to accuse him of the first thought that had leaped into her head. That he—and possibly the whole family—had physically prevented him from coming! Because what work was important enough, she wondered miserably, that a first-time father couldn't take some time out to see his newborn son?

'Luca's been...out of range.'

'Out of range? Out of range of what?' she flung at him

bitterly. 'The planet! The universe! Where have you sent him? Outer Mongolia?'

'I haven't *sent* him anywhere,' he emphasised with unruffled calm.

So it was his father's doing!

'How convenient!' She exhaled, biting back tears, convinced then that keeping Luca from her *was* his family's sole intention.

'I would be more inclined to call it…unfortunate,' he returned, appearing to pick his words carefully. Probably so as not to incriminate himself! Libby wasn't able to help thinking, yet knew a well of immeasurable relief as he told her, 'But we have managed to reach him. He'll be here as soon as he can.'

But not in time to be with her when it had really mattered—when she had really needed him! she thought, trying to excuse his absence, to understand. Deep regret, though, fatigue and the long hours of missing him had robbed her of her ability to be reasonable, and suddenly she was sniping back, 'So in the meantime they've sent you to step into his shoes.'

'Hardly.' The pull of that incredibly masculine mouth made her at once both ashamed and embarrassed at even hinting that this dynamic specimen of manhood might entertain the idea of playing surrogate husband to *her*. And as for trying to suggest that anyone else could dictate his movements, she had to be kidding! 'I did, however, feel it appropriate to bring you these.'

She would never forget her surprise or the lump that rose to her throat as he handed her the bunch of deep crimson roses. She wouldn't forget their scent or their dew-tipped freshness either, but it was the dark brilliance of his eyes as they collided with hers and the husky quality of his voice as he produced those flowers that would remain with her for a long time. That and how mesmerised she felt by the intensity of his dark regard; how she was unable to look away. Then, as a small gurgling sound from the little cot broke the silence between them, 'May I?' he enquired with an assertion that brooked no refusal, because he was already moving around to the other side of the bed.

'You're his uncle,' she said with a little lift of her shoulder beneath her modest cotton nightie, wanting to tag on a grudging, *How can I stop you?* But after that last gesture on his part and that uneasy and silent transmission of something between them, the words wouldn't come.

Instead, she watched with a blend of screaming rejection and fascination as he bent over the cot, saw him clasp a miniature waving pink finger with the strength of his own, and then, uttering a low rumble of welcome to the newest Vincenzo, amazingly he lifted the tiny infant out of his cot, as tenderly as if it were his own.

Watching the emotions chase across his face and reluctantly marvelling at the self-assured confidence beneath that leather-clad frame, she found herself wondering how Romano Vincenzo would treat the woman who had just given him an heir, and knew instinctively that he would have been there for her from the very first twinge, right through her labour, his strength supporting her, until the final moments of birth.

Unaware of how dark she looked under the eyes, or how wildly unkempt her hair was—not until she'd stolen a glance in the bathroom mirror afterwards and found herself wishing that it was anyone but him who had seen her like that—as their eyes clashed over the tiny bundle he was holding, her attention was suddenly drawn to her appearance when he gently commented, 'You look tired, Libby. Has it been a particularly rough ride?'

Exhausted after a difficult labour, vulnerable, aching for Luca, that hint of tenderness in his brother's voice suddenly proved too much.

Tears welled into her eyes, and as her gaze dropped to the perfect little boy that she and Luca had created she clamped her teeth together for fear of revealing any emotion to Romano before, frustrated at her own lack of self-control, she turned shamefully away.

'What's wrong, Libby?' The tenderness was gone, leaving only that cold, incisive edge she knew only too well. 'Haven't things gone in quite the way you'd planned?'

Realisation hit her hard as it dawned on her what he was presuming. That she'd screwed up her face—turned away—because, having married Luca solely for financial gain, the last thing she would want would be to be lumbered with his baby!

She didn't tell him just what she thought—or even attempt to dispel his totally erroneous illusion. Yet afterwards, when he had gone, missing those snatches of concern and gentleness she had glimpsed in him—not just towards Giorgio but also, however unintended, towards her—she cried bitterly.

When he came back again, twelve hours later, it was to break the news to her that Luca was dead.

CHAPTER FIVE

'DON'T you think you're being rather unwise—fraternising with that girl?' The bright morning sunlight streaming in through the long window scored unkind lines across Sophia Vincenzo's face, marring her mature beauty.

'No one's fraternising, Sophia.' Romano's tone was impatient. 'She simply needed help.'

'And you gave it to her.'

He watched her rearranging flowers with her usual ballerina-like grace, remembering how often as a child and a young adult he had wanted to break through that impenetrable exterior; wanted until he had given up.

'What's this all about?'

She didn't look at him as she continued with her arrangement. It had to be perfect. For Sophia, perfection was everything. Or the illusion of perfection at least.

'May I remind you,' she said, 'that your father didn't like her—and with just cause. Oh, I know she's pretty and the stuff of every man's fantasies, but no one rules your heart, Romano—no one ever has. Sometimes I've wondered if you have one—for anyone besides Giorgio, that is.'

Romano's strong teeth clamped together. He didn't relish another pointless argument with Sophia. They had never been close. And, to coin a phrase she had just used herself in relation to Libby, he thought ironically, with just cause.

'I'm going out. Would you like me to do anything for you?' he enquired softly but firmly, hoping to ease the present tension between them. 'Anything in particular?'

'Yes.' Her grey-streaked hair gleamed as she looked up at him now, her eyes cold and clear despite the briefest smile that touched her lips. 'Just remember what she did to my son.'

Her son. His brother. Romano's jaw tightened as he strode out of the room. Luca had been special to her. Her favourite. Sophia had never made any secret of that. He recalled how his brother had needed guiding—watching. Someone in control who could take command over his far too adventurous spirit and try to channel his energies into positive and constructive outlets; rescue him from his own raw and destructive irresponsibility. And Romano, as the elder sibling, he remembered all too painfully, had tried to do that. Over and over and over again.

His business finished, Romano consulted his watch as he moved lithely across the courtyard into the castle. It was two hours since that episode with his mother.

Now, moving through the huge rooms, he found every one deserted; remembered that Sophia had taken Giorgio on a previously arranged coach trip to the coast.

'Why can't Mama come?' the little boy had asked her earnestly when it had been mentioned before dinner the previous evening.

'Because we only have two tickets.' His grandmother's reply had brooked no argument. It was clear, Romano thought, that Sophia had had no intention of relinquishing a day with her grandson to his long-estranged mother, or even to attempt to see if another ticket could be arranged.

Libby might not rank very highly in his mother's opinion. Or indeed, he thought drily, in his own. But he had felt a rare degree of sympathy for her when, obviously having interpreted all that was being said, she had put an arm around Giorgio and said she hoped he'd enjoy it, hiding her disappointment behind a brave little smile.

Now, having tossed down his briefcase and jacket, slipped off his tie and enquired of a member of staff where she could be, it was with a smug satisfaction that he headed for the garden, realising that for the first time since he had brought Libby back here he was going to have her all to himself.

With Giorgio gone for the day, Libby hadn't realised how much she would miss him. It was as though a limb had been torn from her, she thought, and she didn't know what to do.

She had wandered out here into the garden to lose herself amongst the vibrant shrubs and quiet pathways that were all part of Romano's new and very aesthetically planned landscaping, to try and walk off the restlessness that had plagued her inside.

Some things hadn't changed, she noticed, picking out the statues and tall, tapering cypress trees she recognised from when she had lived there before.

She stopped dead suddenly, inhaling the honey-scented pink spikes of a huge bush that was growing near the path.

Her butterfly bush! she remembered with a stab of something painfully acute. Luca had brought it home for her one day—just a small shrub in a pot—knowing how much she'd wanted one. That was one of the less detrimental reasons why he'd started calling her 'his butterfly girl'. He'd said it was a token of his love and that he would plant it for her, but in the end he hadn't got around to it, and she had had to do it alone. As she'd found herself doing everything with increasing regularity, a cruel little voice inside suddenly piped up to taunt her. Alone.

Oh, he had been full of high ideas and good intentions, Libby reminded herself with a sad little smile in his defence. And his few faults, of course, had paled into insignificance beneath the weight of loss and grief she had suffered after his accident. Yet now, watching a colony of red admirals flitting appreciatively over the bright crimson blooms that wreathed gracefully curving branches, she was forced to accept that planting her butterfly bush was just one of those intentions that had never came to fruition.

"We'll do it together," he'd resorted to saying when she had given him one or two gentle reminders. Over three weeks later, when it was looking sad and pot-bound on one of the lesser used balconies, she had taken it herself and found a spade after the gardeners had finished for the day, and tried, without much success, to penetrate the hard, baked earth.

She hadn't even been aware of Romano's approach. Not until he was standing right next to her and, without a word, had taken the spade out of her hands.

Surprised and disconcerted by his presence, she'd looked on as, dressed in the immaculate dark suit he'd worn to the office, he'd forced the earth to yield beneath his expensive black shoe, and driven the spade effortlessly into the ground.

He still hadn't spoken as she shook the tangled little plant free of its confining pot, loosening its strangled roots. Not until he had refilled the hole with an economical wielding of the spade and she'd patted the freshly dug earth firmly down with her bare hands.

'Nurture it,' he'd advised succinctly then. 'Like husbands, they require a little attention now and again if you're to reap all the rewards you're clearly hoping for.'

'Thanks for the tip,' she'd said sarcastically, knowing he was referring to her frequent and increasingly long visits to England and what he saw as an escape from the confines of her inconvenient marriage. They hadn't known—any of them! she thought, with emotion welling up inside of her—how much she adored Luca, and yet how increasingly like an outcast she had been made to feel.

'So this is where you are!'

His deep voice made her jump and, swiping at her wet cheeks, Libby swung round, struck by that feeling of *déjà vu* he'd commented on the day he brought her back.

'It's cooler here.' Her words came out on a shaky little croak because she hadn't expected to see him; because he had caught her at a particularly vulnerable moment and, from the furrow deepening between his eyes, he was fully aware of it.

'Much.' He glanced up at the welcome canopy of narrow green leaves and dense, spiky flowers, causing Libby to wonder if he too was remembering their joint efforts that day so long ago.

'It lived—without my being here to nurture it,' she quietly reminded him and guessed that he was probably supplementing an unvoiced 'so there!' although she hadn't intended to sound in any way smug. All that was in her mind right now was how stupendously masculine he looked with an open-necked white shirt accentuating his tan and pale grey trousers hugging every hard angle of his lower body so that she could feel every feminine cell zinging in response to it.

'Buddleja davidii,' he quoted, reminding her of its Latin name. 'It's thoroughly invasive and will take over the garden if you let it. Nevertheless, it's a beautiful specimen and butterflies are addicted to it.' As he could so easily become addicted to her, he warned himself brutally, wondering what was stopping him from pulling the pins out of the swept-up hair that exposed her enticing neck and shoulders and dragging her into his arms, feel her warm, pliant body beneath that virginal white sundress pressing against every hard, pulsing sinew of his. 'Attributed to a French priest…' somehow he managed to force himself to concentrate on a far safer subject, ignore the burning ache in his groin '…who also discovered the giant panda, which is, unfortunately, one of his less productive discoveries.'

A bubble of laughter burst from Libby. 'Are you always such a mine of useless information?' she enquired cheekily.

'It's a topical subject.' A smile touched his mouth. A mouth which only hours before had been driving her crazy for him, Libby thought shamefully, banishing the humiliating memory of it fiercely from her mind. 'Giorgio has been learning about him at school.'

'Did he teach you all that?' she laughed, more tensely this time.

Romano shrugged. 'From the mouths of babes.'

Libby nodded. They could teach you a lot, she thought. Only she'd been denied the chance of learning anything from her young son.

'You've spent a lot of time with him, haven't you?'

It was the closest thing to admitting that she had watched those cassettes and that she had behaved badly and ungraciously when he had left them in her room. But even alluding to last night after what had transpired between them brought embarrassed colour to her cheeks and, unsettled by his dark, all too knowing scrutiny, she had to look away, pretend an interest in a large peacock butterfly that had settled just above her head, the bright circles on its wings quite conspicuously blue.

'Someone had to,' the sudden change in Romano's tone chilled her like a cold wind, 'the child having been robbed of both a father and a mother.'

Libby's head jerked back, the accusation in her eyes vying with the palpable condemnation she could see burning in his. 'And what are you saying? That it was all my fault?'

The sun filtering through the yellow leaves of an *Acer* tree growing behind the butterfly bush slashed harsh shadows across Romano's face. He didn't answer. He didn't have to! Libby thought, peeved.

'Oh, I know exactly what you think of me, Romano!' Arms folded as though to protect herself from some invisible attack, she brushed purposely past him, intent on heading back towards the equally harsh austerity of his home. 'I know that to you I'm just an avaricious little gold-digger who saw your brother as an easy target!' she threw back over her shoulder, aware of his hounding footsteps right behind her.

'Wasn't he?'

She sliced him a hard, deprecating look as he caught up with her.

Too big. Too commanding. Too powerful. The type of man who struck awe into the hearts of lesser men and an overwhelming excitement into those of most women! Herself included! she thought despairingly.

'To someone who might have been hoping to take him for every penny they could get—yes, he was,' she agreed. 'He was a little bit naïve in that respect and generous to a fault.' All too well she recalled the gifts he had lavished upon her. Jewellery. Designer clothes. An extortionately priced car she hadn't been at all sure he could afford.

'Generous to a fault, *si*, and would have been more so, no doubt, if the money he had inherited from his grandfather hadn't been safely withheld from him until his twenty-fifth birthday.' Because Luca had been a fool with money. And not just with her, but with his friends, too. Most of them opportunists—nothing but hangers-on, she remembered unhappily.

'But I didn't need that money, did I?' she reminded his brother bitterly, exasperated by his eternal implications. 'Not when I could use Giorgio as a bargaining tool to get it out of your father instead!' An angry glance at him revealed the taut lines of his cheek and jaw, and the granite-hard firmness of his mouth. And suddenly, frustrated by his inexorable refusal to see her for who she really was, she burst out, 'You're just a narrow-minded bigot, Romano Vincenzo! Good grief! You must really hate me if you still believe a thing like that!'

Which was the wrong thing to say, she realised at once when, catching her arm, he suddenly pulled her round to face him.

'And does it matter, my beautiful grieving widow…' his scything words didn't quite tally with the husky quality of his voice '…whether I hate you or not?'

It did. Heaven knew! She didn't know why! But it did!

The pulsing strength of his masculinity seemed to be igniting her blood, the elusive scent of his cologne weakening her resolve after last night to resist the dangerous pull of whatever it was between them that overrode resentment, dislike or even—as he'd suggested—hate.

'Of course not!' she breathed, and pulled angrily out of his grasp. 'Only that any human being should think me so unscrupulous!'

'I've seen no evidence to the contrary,' Romano said, pursuing her despite her attempts to shrug him off, wondering why he no longer felt the full weight of his convictions. Was it because of those tears he had witnessed a moment ago when he had caught her off-guard? Or because of the surprising yet unmistakable depth of feeling she had for Giorgio? Perhaps Sophia was right, he speculated grimly. Perhaps he *was* allowing the effects of this girl's soft femininity to rule his head.

Driven by that thought, and by the mental imagery that always kicked in hard whenever he felt his defences being weakened by her, he ground out, 'And you seem to have forgotten, *cara,* but I haven't. That night I saw you during one of your many sojourns to England. Pregnant with my brother's child and— what is the expression?—living it up under the pretext of playing nursemaid to your father, while Luca was safely and conveniently out of the way here in Italy!'

'That's not true!' Libby defended herself, hot colour staining her cheeks, creeping down her throat. 'And I didn't keep going back because I had some clandestine lover I'd left at home—as I'm well aware you were all too ready to believe! My father *was* ill! He had nobody else to care for him and I couldn't leave him on his own! When you saw me that night at the country club it was only because people had been keeping on at me—telling me I should take a night off, go out for an evening. I was exhausted! Worn down with the strain and worry of Dad and torn in two by split loyalties! Trying to do what was best for him and be fair to Luca! Even my doctor told me I should take a break! And the only time I gave in and got a friend to sit in for Dad—allowed myself a few hours' recreation—I had to bump slam-bang right into you!'

'Which was rather unfortunate, wasn't it, *carissima...*' Despite the endearment, as he fell into step beside her again condemnation oozed out of every superb inch of him '...as it turned out?'

'Why?' She stopped dead on the path. 'Because I was on the dance floor with a man who happened to be the husband of a neighbour I really liked and respected?' Her bright head came up as she faced him with pulsing indignation. 'Who also happened to be there with us that night!'

She could tell that beneath that hard, implacable exterior he was quietly but very thoroughly shaken.

'Santo cielo!' he breathed after a few moments. 'You cannot blame me for leaping to the obvious conclusion. The way you were dancing that night there wasn't a man at that club who could keep his eyes off you!'

A lizard ran across the path, a flash of movement, one moment there—the next gone, swallowed up in a thicket of lush undergrowth.

'Including you, by the sound of it!' Her blood raced from the possibility that she might have affected him in that way, though she had seen only anger glittering in his incredible eyes.

Including him, Romano acknowledged, his breath catching in his lungs.

It had incensed him to watch her dancing with the man he'd believed was her lover. But he couldn't forget that other emotion he was ready to admit now was irrational jealousy as he'd watched the way she'd moved beneath a not particularly flattering dress, her hair swaying like a sensuous red curtain, her body made voluptuous by pregnancy. Not that anyone would have realised had they not been aware of it already, he thought, because her condition hadn't shown until it was quite advanced.

'You were married to my brother!' he rasped, as though that could negate the unforgivable feelings that had tormented him whenever he was around her. Desire. Wanting. Need. But it went far deeper than that. Her intelligence, her beauty and her gentle manner were in themselves an ensnaring combination. But it was the way she quietly stood up to not just his parents, but him too—deflecting his caustic comments with guarded tolerance one minute, and open challenge the next—that tugged at some crazy reluctant regard for her deep inside of him. And that only intensified his mindless desire for her and his increasing guilt, a vicious circle of feelings he could only handle by staying away from the castle. He was almost glad when she lived up to everything he had believed her to be.

'Yes, I *was* married to your brother and I asked him to come and join me! Not leave me there on my own to cope alone with Dad. I kept asking him to come.' Begging him, she remembered, only she didn't say that. 'I wanted him to, but he could just never get away. You and Sophia and Marius made sure of that. He said he'd be made to feel he was shirking his responsibilities. Letting the company and the so-called *family* down if he tore himself away for just a week or two to be with his wife!' *And then there was his mammoth allowance that he suddenly started caring about losing,* but she didn't say that either. 'He knew all he'd wind up getting would be recriminations and disapproval from his wonderful family—including you,' she finished pointedly, 'if he had!'

A breeze swept up from the coast, ruffling Romano's hair into a sea of ebony ripples. Those glittering eyes boring into hers seemed to Libby to be stripping her to her bare bones.

She saw a shadow flit across his face, a dark emotion as though he was having some sort of inner battle with himself.

'Come on,' he said, catching her hand.

The small plane seemed to glide over the magnificent bay. Below them Naples sprawled like a sweltering red jungle. Intense buildings. Congested roads. And mighty archeological ruins. To the west, cruise ships floated like white palaces in the harbour, presided over by an ancient fortress, a legacy of less peaceful times. Above it all Mount Vesuvius towered like a slumbering cone-shaped monster. Powerful. Destructive. Magnificent.

'Don't worry. It's not going to erupt—at least not today,' Romano assured her wryly, noticing where her interest lay. 'If that's what you're thinking.' Which was the only thing that wasn't, he thought, if he let his feelings for this girl run riot.

'I wasn't,' she answered, considering the violent act of nature that had devastated this area and its population nearly two thousand years ago. 'I was thinking it reminded me of you.'

'Me?' He laughed. 'No, don't tell me!' he said, putting up his hand. 'Let me guess. Big, imposing and with a tendency to getting far too overheated where present company is concerned?'

His reminder of the previous night brought shaming colour to her cheeks so that she glanced away, down at the hub of the bustling city way below them. How could he fly this thing? Stay so composed? she wondered, impressed by his capability while discussing something so intimately disturbing as sex!

'Why not add outlandishly conceited to that?' she said, but couldn't help laughing nevertheless. How had he managed to make her feel like this?

With long-acquired skill he manoeuvred the aircraft seaward, leaving the coast curving in a wide golden arc behind them. 'Because it wouldn't be true.'

Her snort of scepticism drew an amused masculine glance her way.

'At least I've got you to relax,' he said on a more serious note. 'To smile for a change.'

'Is that why you brought me up here? Just to witness a rare re-arrangement of my features?'

'I don't have to propel us both skyward to do that,' he remarked drily, so that she felt her cheeks colouring again, aware exactly what he was hinting at. 'I thought you could do with some fun.'

'Fun?' An elevated eyebrow mockingly challenged that idea. 'With you?'

'Is that such an unimaginable concept?'

'Yes,' she stressed, but laughed again in spite of herself, envying his proficiency as a pilot. She was not only trusting this man with her life, she realised suddenly, but felt perfectly at ease in doing so too, and was comfortable in the silence that ensued as he navigated the plane across the indigo water.

'So...Elizabeth Vincenzo...' he didn't see her flinch, or realise how his sidelong glance at her made her blood race when those dark-fringed eyes made a swift but assessing survey of her body '...how do you like to enjoy yourself? When you aren't driving men crazy with those big green eyes and that fiery hair?'

What was that supposed to mean? Libby mused, catching her breath. Was he presuming that because of last night and that night in her flat that she was sex-mad? she thought, wondering what he would say if she told him she hadn't been to bed with a man since his brother had died. He'd probably laugh, or at the very least think she was telling lies.

Choosing to ignore his disconcerting remark, above the drone of the engine she said soberly, 'I was made to promise never to use that name.'

'Scusi?'

'Vincenzo,' she elaborated. As if he needed reminding! Denied her, she remembered bitingly, because his father could still have carried out his unspeakable threat if she hadn't done exactly as she'd been ordered to do. 'I didn't want to give it up. I was Luca's widow. I had a right to it. That's why I took the English form of Vincent. It wasn't hurting anyone. I still had my married name in a way, although I wasn't sullying yours by degrading the name of one of the oldest and most respected families in Italy!' She couldn't keep the sarcasm out of her voice, or the accusation as she tagged on, 'Anyway, I thought you played a role in all those...conditions.'

He engaged the controls as ahead of them the Isle of Capri beckoned, a sun-baked pleasure island above the glittering sea.

'What *conditions?*' His voice was deceptively soft.

Libby darted a less than amiable glance his way. He had to be joking surely? 'The ones your father laid down when he forced me into giving up my son!'

'My father *forced* you into handing over Giorgio?' His concentration was split now between his handling of the plane and what she was telling him. Even so, she knew she was perfectly safe. 'What are you saying?'

Hurting, puzzled, Libby looked at him in disbelief. How could he pretend not to know?

'I didn't hand Giorgio over, Romano,' she decided to remind him anyway. 'Not in the way you prefer to believe I did. I was ill after I'd had him and couldn't come back for Luca's funeral. When I did manage to get here, your parents told me they wanted to adopt Giorgio. They were pleasant about it at first, but when they could see that I wasn't prepared to give him up they made me do it under duress.'

'But…you were paid…handsomely…made terms which you agreed to…'

His puzzled reminder had her looking away and gritting her teeth to stem the anger and pain that were suddenly welling up inside her. 'Oh, I was paid off all right!'

'How? For what reason does a mother part with her baby if it is entirely against her wishes to do so?'

'Through a gradual wearing down and a stronger will—bulked up by a much bigger bank balance! Your father owned the cottage we lived in—that your grandfather still allowed us to live in rent-free after he'd been forced to give up work. It had been Dad's home for most of his life. In the end, when Marius could see I was adamant about keeping Giorgio—stubborn, he called it—he threatened to evict him. The doctors said a move at that time would almost certainly kill Dad, and your father knew that. He also knew that if it didn't destroy him physically, then it would grieve him so much to leave his home that he would probably have died of a broken heart. I didn't want the money he was offering, but I thought if I refused it he would have seen it as an act of insurgence on my part—that I wasn't keeping to my side of the bargain. I was afraid for Dad.'

He didn't say anything as they approached the island's airfield, negotiating the runway to land the small aircraft with smooth and effortless skill.

She had never seen him look so darkly forbidding. If he'd looked shaken before, his face appeared bloodless now, making his angular features as hard as the rocky coast over which they had just flown.

'If you think I helped engineer a plot like that…' he spoke very quietly, but she could feel the anger in him bubbling just beneath the surface '…then you don't know me very well. Something, *mia cara*, we are going to have to rectify—as of now!'

CHAPTER SIX

'I'VE never been to Capri,' Libby remarked, surprising herself as well as Romano as she gazed with delighted eyes from the rear seat of the chauffeur-driven car that had meet them at the airport, taking it all in. The tiny squares—bustling with day-trippers. The flower-decked white houses and the narrow alleyways of the island's principal town perched high on the rugged cliffs above the sea. 'Not even through my work,' she added, although her job had taken her to many exotic places over the years.

'Then you have a treat in store,' he told her, looking decidedly pleased as he caught her hand, linking his fingers with hers as though it were the most natural thing in the world; as though they hadn't been enemies for the past seven years until reaching some point of amnesty up there in the sky; as though it didn't produce the same riot of sensations in him that ran chaotically in Libby as the action caused her fingers to brush against the hard strength of his thigh.

But he was right. Being on Capri was a treat, she decided when they were sipping cappuccinos outside a street café in a pedestrian thoroughfare, flanked one side with flowering oleander trees, the other sporting a profusion of matching white bell-shaped canopies above the doorways of designer boutiques.

'So…is this not every woman's dream?' Romano smiled, indicating the shops with their temptingly dressed windows as he tucked into a slice of the mouth-zinging lemon cake that they had both decided to order with their coffee.

'And every husband's nightmare, I should imagine!' she laughed, well aware of the sort of price tag the clothes in those shops carried. She hadn't come so far, though, that she had forgotten the value of things and how hard it could be to struggle with hardly enough money to live on. She hoped she never would.

'You said you lost your father recently,' Romano commented, seeming to pick up on the line her thoughts had taken, 'and your mother…when you were an infant, I believe.'

She had never told him that, so he must have got it from Luca and remembered it, Libby surmised, guessing that very little would be lost from this man's clever mind once it was firmly lodged there.

She nodded.

'That must have been hard,' he empathised.

She gave a little shrug of acceptance. 'We coped.'

'So what did you do when you walked out of our lives? Before taking up your career as one of the planet's loveliest models?'

You mean before I was pushed out? she wanted to remind him, but stopped herself in time. They had handed each other the metaphorical olive branch earlier. She didn't want to be the one to allow it to snap.

Her shoulder lifted again in light dismissal of his casually delivered compliment. She had been called beautiful on countless occasions, but coming from him it filled her with heart-warming pleasure.

'I took business studies,' she told him, 'at home, so that I could be around to help Dad. The modelling happened quite by chance. I hadn't planned to do it, but Dad had found a new partner—one of the nurses when he was in hospital—and he insisted I made the most of the opportunity and he supported—no, *pushed* me' she amended fondly, 'every step of the way.'

'He must have been proud of his daughter—and of her devotion to him.'

She gave that familiar little shrug he was getting used to

whenever he said anything that was remotely flattering, as though complimenting her on her attributes and achievements embarrassed her. She was looking choked up, though, he noticed, and guessed that he was probing wounds that were still too raw.

'So why did you never try to get Giorgio back?'

His question, across the top of his cappuccino, surprised her.

'I did,' she responded, setting her own cup down, her spirit returning as she reiterated fiercely, 'Believe me, I did!'

'And?'

'And access—let alone any chance of custody—was firmly denied. By the time I'd started to earn money so that your father's threats couldn't have hurt Dad, they'd already adopted Giorgio legally. I wrote him letters but they were returned. They wouldn't even let me send him birthday cards without sending them back.'

He remembered that buckled card he'd noticed in the drawer last night and was fuelled by a sudden propulsion of anger towards his parents.

'I really didn't know any of this.' Whatever else she thought about him, it was suddenly absolutely vital to make that clear to her. 'I was abroad for a period. No one told me what was going on.'

'So what about you?'

He laughed. 'What about me?' He was glad she had changed the subject. It was difficult coming to terms with what his parents had done.

'Apart from boarding-school and university, playing squash and swimming, what have you done besides save a retail chain, turn the fortunes of an airline around and earn yourself the title of "youngest billionaire" in last year's Rich List?' she enquired, eager to learn what it was that really made him tick.

He laughed again before finishing his cappuccino. 'That's about it,' he accepted with a wry attempt at immodesty, his earlier suggestion that she should get to know him better obviously not something she was going to achieve over coffee. 'Well…' setting down his cup, he gestured towards the boutiques '…are you going to let an opportunity like this bypass you?'

Amusement tugged at Libby's mouth. 'In England we say "pass you by",' she corrected, her eyes drawn to the balconies above the shops where geranium-filled baskets blazed with a riot of colour. 'But if you think a spell of retail therapy and wallowing in designer clothes is how I like to spend my time, then you don't know me very well either,' she assured him softly.

'Oh?'

Why did the full impact of his gaze have the power to make her blood tingle?

She swallowed, trying to control the feeling. 'My idea of total relaxation is just to go walking in the countryside,' she said, 'just to be away from the noise and the traffic and everything about the city, and to be able to hear just the birds and insects and the wind in the trees instead. That's a pleasure no amount of spending can equal.' She saw his mouth quirk almost sardonically. 'What's wrong?' she challenged, suddenly defensive. 'Doesn't that quite tally with the materialistic person you thought I was?'

Almost imperceptibly his shoulder moved. 'You just surprise me—every step of the way.'

'You mean I'm one step ahead of you.'

Resting on the white tablecloth, his long brown hands opened in unconditional acceptance. 'So I've got some catching up to do.'

Was that his way of admitting that he'd been wrong?

'Prejudiced people are usually surprised—if they allow themselves to be.'

Romano's jaws clamped tightly together. She had forced him to see that he had been prejudiced all right! And now she was turning the screw. It didn't help any telling himself that he deserved her soft reprobation. Deeply, however, with the richness of melting chocolate, he murmured, 'So surprise me some more.'

Across the table Libby felt herself responding to his lazily seductive voice with a pooling of heat deep down in her lower body.

Would it surprise him to know that he just had to look at her to make her blood run with a molten heat that made Naples' famous volcano seem as tame as a Baked Alaska? That when she was in his company she was a mixture of so many conflicting emotions she didn't know who she was, or even if she liked herself? How could she, she ruminated, when she allowed a man who thought so little of her—and whom she disliked in turn—to ensnare her with his irrepressible sexuality, storm her defences in the way he did?

Tautly muscled, superbly lean and broad-shouldered as he was, it wasn't just *her* eyes that were drawn to his strong, intensely masculine physique. Every woman who had passed along the street since they had been sitting there had spared him more than just one glance. And why not? she thought, realising that she was as feeble as they were because she couldn't tug her eyes away from him. He looked rich, virile and handsome, but it was a handsomeness overlaid with that air of authority that drew people's attention to him, in the sweep of his high, intellectual forehead and his proud, straight nose, in his firm, determined mouth and his forceful jaw.

And she was just as feeble as all the rest of them! Libby thought, because she couldn't tear her gaze away from him no matter how hard she tried.

Above their sun umbrella the oleander trees exuded their powdery scent, which, with the other exotic smells that seemed to surround her on this pleasure island, was making her head swim in a mix of heady perfume. Suddenly she was experiencing a rare and dizzying lightness of heart and was glad that he had brought her here today.

Caught in the snare of his dark gaze, she saw his black brows come together, grasped the small curse he uttered under his breath.

'This wasn't a very good idea.'

He should have taken her somewhere else, he thought, somewhere where they could have been entirely alone—not mistakenly believed that because she was a model she would throw abandon to the shops like most of the women he knew; women who were only interested in how they looked and continually needed to feed their egos to that end.

'It was yours,' she reminded him, in a voice that quavered. What was he saying? That he didn't want to be here with her after all?

'We all make mistakes,' he said. 'And before you tell me—I know. I've made a few.'

'A *few?*' A bit of an understatement, she thought, although with a man as proud as Romano was she couldn't expect a total climb-down all in one day. She wondered, though, why he had had sudden reservations about being there with her. Why he courted this unmistakable and dangerous attraction between them and yet seemed to condemn himself for it at the same time. Did he still think her unfit to grace the world he inhabited, even though she had tried to convince him she wasn't the person he thought she was? Or was there some other reason for the self-castigating way he had cursed himself just now? Like the chic Italian girl she'd been unable to miss laughing with Giorgio in the most recent of those videos she had watched last night. A woman she had heard Romano referring to as Magdelena in the silkily honeyed tones of a lover.

'Why are you looking so sorry for yourself suddenly?' Romano's eyes were far too discerning as they probed the guarded green of hers.

'I was wondering if you were going to show me the rest of the island,' she parried.

He gestured to the waiter hovering in the doorway of the café.

'If it takes that haunted look out of your eyes and assures me that my efforts won't be wasted, I'll make you a gift of Herculaneum,' he promised, after requesting the bill. He meant the remains of the ancient Roman city over which they had flown earlier, devastated by the volcanic ash that had also claimed Pompeii.

'OK, you're powerful,' she laughed, trying to banish an image of a sleek black bob, sparkling black eyes and petite femininity, 'but not that powerful!' Not unless you were talking about his influence among the kings of commerce and industry, or the sensual paradise to which she was sure a woman would find herself transported from the unquestionable expertise of his lovemaking. Because he would be experienced in the art of pleasuring a woman, she was certain of that.

'Put it away,' he said, seeing her reaching for her purse after the waiter had reappeared, leaving their bill.

'I like to go Dutch when I'm with a man,' she informed him candidly, face flushed, her voice a little husky from her unwitting thoughts just now.

'Too bad. You're in Italy now,' he reminded her with a cordial smile, though his eyes defied her to argue. 'And I'm not just any man. I'm your—'

He broke off as a shout from across the paved walkway claimed both their attention. My what? Libby thought, wondering what he had been going to say. Her brother-in-law? Her host? The official guardian of her child? Or was she really hoping that he could be something much more intimate than that?

'Romano!' A tall, elderly man had come out of the café and was striding towards their table. *'Romano! Buono giorno!'* He slapped Romano on the shoulder as he got to his feet, giving his hand a firm and lengthy shake.

'Teodoro is the café owner and an old acquaintance of the family,' Romano paused from a mutual roll of fast flowing and almost totally incomprehensible Italian to tell her. He said something else to the older man, something that made the proprietor appraise her with openly admiring eyes as Romano introduced her, having no qualms about using her rightful name, she noted, wondering why even such a tiny measure of acceptance by him should make her ache for something inside, make her nerve-endings quiver as her eyes clashed with the glittering ebony of his.

'So you are Luca's young widow.' She wasn't sure what Romano had told him, but it wasn't that. On her feet, she smiled up at this likeable Italian, who took the hand she offered, pressing it to his lips. 'We met once,' he said in his thickly accented voice, 'at the Castle Vincenzo. You probably do not remember.' Which she didn't, Libby realised, bluffing her way out of having to actually admit as much by giving him one of her naturally warm yet mesmerising types of smile that cameramen all over the world had fallen in love with. It explained, though, how he knew who she was. 'Such a tragedy.' She guessed it was because he hadn't been able to offer her his condolences at the time that he made such a point of doing so now. 'So young.' He was shaking his silver-grey head. 'They were both so young.'

Libby's smile faltered as her fine brows came together. 'I'm sorry?' She shot a questioning glance towards Romano.

He uttered something very terse to Teodoro. He looked, Libby thought, in a hurry to get away.

'No! No! *Per favore!*' Picking up the notes Romano had tossed down on top of the bill, Teodoro was pressing them back into his hand.

'Grazias.' A fleeting smile from Romano, a reciprocal slap on the back and he was urging Libby away from their table as though he had a train to catch.

'What did he mean,' she quizzed, trying to keep up with him as they turned down into one of the quieter, tree-fringed streets, still puzzling over what Teodoro had said, 'about the accident? He said "they".'

Romano was barking some sort of order into his cellphone, his face surprisingly grim. 'You misheard him?'

'No, I didn't.' She had never been so certain of anything in her life. 'Was there someone else in the car with Luca that day? Did he have a passenger?'

'Yes.'

'No one ever told me that. Why not?' And incredulously, 'Why didn't you tell me?' she persisted, her eyes mystified, hurt.

He didn't answer as he slipped his phone back into his trouser pocket.

'Was it a woman?' she demanded of his dark, forbidding profile. 'Was it?'

'Yes.' His reply was snatched.

'Who?'

'Just some girl.'

'Some girl? Who? Who was she? A hitchhiker?'

'I believe she was an executive from one of the companies Luca was dealing with.'

'An executive…' She broke off, her chest rising sharply beneath the simple sundress. There was an innocent explanation. There had to be. Why, then, was he being so cagey? 'Were they…? Was he…?' *Having an affair?* Her eyes demanded an answer even though her tongue couldn't bring herself to ask it. *Not Luca. Please, not Luca!* she prayed.

Romano shook his head, not in negation, she realised, but in frustration because he hadn't wanted to tell her.

'Oh, *no!*' She turned and moved away from him, her arms wrapped tightly around her body as though in that way she would somehow be protected from the truth.

'Libby…' Romano's hand was gentle on her shoulder, but forcefully she flung it away.

'Leave me alone!'

'Libby!' He came purposefully after her, pulled her to face him. 'I'm sorry. I didn't want you to find out this way.'

'No?' She was shivering, he noticed, despite the heat, and there were bitter tears making her eyes glitter like emerald pools. 'In what way were you going to tell me? Or weren't you? Leave her in the dark and let someone else do it! My husband was having an affair when he died, so why not keep it from me and let one of your friends tell me instead?'

'It wasn't like that,' he stressed. 'Teodoro didn't know. As far as the outside world was concerned, Luca died with a colleague who happened to be involved in the same deal as he was, which would have accounted for why they were travelling together that morning.'

Because Vincenzo money could pay for anything—even the

privacy they guarded so jealously, Libby accepted, torn by the revelation of Luca's unbelievable betrayal.

'Even Sophia didn't know.' His father had seen to that, Romano thought. Sworn him to secrecy, he remembered.

'Why not? Wasn't anything allowed to tarnish the reputation of their favourite son?'

She didn't see the way Romano flinched at her remark, nor did she absorb anything of her surroundings—a couple walking past them with a dog; the exclusive private villas that ran the length of the street; how the bright pinks of the oleander trees made a stark and pleasing contrast against the diamond-hard blue of the sky.

'I didn't think it would matter very much to you. I thought his playing around was some sort of defence mechanism against something that he was too proud to tell me. That things weren't working out between the two of you. I thought you'd driven him to it. *Santo cielo!* You were enough to drive any man insane!'

'And that invalidated my right to know? He was my *husband!*' she tossed at him grievously.

Turning her back on him, she was unaware of the car that purred silently to a halt alongside the pavement until strong hands on her shoulders were urging her to step in.

'I don't want to go anywhere with you,' she breathed, not sure whom she wanted to lash out at most—him or his brother. Or even herself for being such a blind, trusting and totally gullible fool.

The disquieting sound of the door closing behind them told her that her wishes were way down on the agenda. The Romanos of this world got what they wanted, however, whenever and wherever they chose!

The car pulled away without any instruction to the driver. He would already be *au fait* with his employer's wishes, Libby thought, sitting there in numb silence. She couldn't believe it. How could Luca have done this to her? she agonised. She'd thought he appreciated why she had to keep going back to England. She'd thought he understood…

'I loved him.' Her voice was a small squeak, stifled by the pain of her discovery.

Beside her Romano dragged in a shuddering breath. Wasn't he already beginning to work that out for himself? It was too soon to tell her that, though. To have to openly admit that on yet another point he had been wrong. Instead, all he said heavily was, 'So did I.'

'He wanted to be like you,' she murmured, staring straight ahead at the thick neck and wide shoulders of the man he had earlier referred to as Miguel behind the screening glass partition. 'He said he felt overshadowed by everything you did. Everything you were. That was why he was the way he was. Always looking for excitement. Being a bit crazy…' Not finding it in the arms of other women. Deceiving her. Pretending she was so special when in fact she had meant very little to him at all.

'He didn't need to,' Romano said quietly. 'He was indulged at every feasible level.'

'By you?'

'No, not by me. I was merely the safety net. The one having to pick up the pieces. Bail him out of trouble. Constantly. Because of his hare-brained ideas of having fun. His irresponsibility with money. Even his relationships.'

Stiffly, Libby half turned to face him now. 'Were there others?' she whispered, not knowing whether she could bear it if he told her that there were. 'Were there others while he was married to me?'

Long sable lashes came down, the tautness of his jaw showing her how much it probably pained him to remember his brother like this, and it was several seconds before he replied.

'Not that I know of.' His hesitation could have meant he was shielding her from further pain, but somehow Libby knew he was telling her the truth. He was hard-headed, didn't suffer fools and in business had a reputation for being quite ruthless. But he also had a reputation for being fair and instinctively she knew that, unlike his younger brother—the man she had given her heart to, and who had just driven a stake through it when she had learned of his deception until she felt as though she was bleeding inside—Romano Vincenzo would never lie.

Tell me one thing—' she was staring straight ahead again, seeing nothing but the past '—that night you couldn't find him—the night I had Giorgio—had you been looking for him?'

'Yes.'

'Where was he?'

'In some log cabin somewhere.'

'With her?'

He didn't answer. He didn't need to, she thought, lapsing into silence, because really, what else was there to say?

'Come on.' His low command mobilised her into realising how much time must have passed, because it wasn't until then that she noticed that the car had stopped.

They had arrived at some luxurious and quiet retreat. A contemporary white villa of modern Moorish design, with arched porticoes supported by fine twisted marble columns, set in luxuriant grounds where palm trees stirred gently in the scented breeze.

Like an automaton Libby allowed him to lead her inside.

Wide and striking interior white arches linked open and airy spaces, where pale marble columns, pale rugs and tasteful watercolour paintings lent a whisper of colour to its white walls and tiled floor. A wide sweeping staircase with wrought-iron curlicues followed the contemporary design of the living space, where exquisitely patterned tiles on each vertical rise added dramatic splashes of colour to the villa's minimalist style.

She gave a mirthless little laugh. 'Just another of your homes?'

'My principal home. Or it will be,' he added, 'when I marry.'

When I marry.

His words intruded sharply on her numbed senses.

Of course, she thought. He would marry at some stage. He was far too eligible and too darned attractive to remain single forever.

Is it imminent? Though the words flew to her brain, they stopped dead on her tongue. She didn't want to know. Didn't want any more unwelcome surprises today. One was enough, she thought wretchedly. Anyway, what did it matter? Why should she care? She didn't. The only reason she was here in Italy was because of Giorgio.

'Libby…'

'Don't.' She put up her hands in negation of whatever he was going to say. 'I don't want to talk about it. I don't want to talk about anything,' she cautioned, feeling exhausted.

'Can I get you something to eat?'

Wearily, she shook her head. Learning about her son's father had obviously come as a total shock—thoroughly draining her, Romano observed shrewdly. There was a whiteness to the skin beneath the wells of her eyes and around her mouth, and several strands of her bright hair had escaped from its casually tied knot.

'I'd just like to be alone for a while.'

He didn't say anything, just indicated for her to precede him up the stairs.

The suite into which he showed her boasted the same sense of airiness and space as the areas downstairs, from its pale walls and white-canopied wrought-iron four-poster bed to the fine, exclusive modern ornaments and the gauzy curtains that were moving gently in the afternoon breeze.

The view from one of the windows beyond the balcony would in other circumstances have quite literally taken her breath away as, way off in the distance, she glimpsed the jutting shape of the Sorrento peninsula, flanked on one side by the wide and glittering Bay of Naples, and on the other by the sweeping, sun-bathed gold of the Gulf of Salerno.

She failed to derive any pleasure from it now.

How could he? she agonised, tormented by what she had learned about Luca. How could he have pretended? Led her on to believe that he'd loved her as much as she'd loved him when all the time he was cheating on her, finding pleasure in another woman's arms even as she was giving birth to their beautiful baby?

Bitter tears stung her eyes and, turning away from the window, she flung herself down onto the sensuous bed and cried until she could cry no more.

She felt sticky and her dress was crumpled when she woke up what seemed hours later. A glance at the slim silver watch on her wrist, though, revealed that she had only slept for just over forty minutes.

Needing to freshen up, she glanced into the luxurious adjacent bathroom. She was longing for a shower but she'd dropped her bag, with her comb and the change of underwear she had been trained through her job always to carry, somewhere downstairs when she had come in.

She found Romano sitting on one of the white sofas in the magnificently arched living area working with his laptop on a low table in front of him. He looked up as she stepped quietly down off the last curving stair and retrieved her bag from another table near the door.

'Is it all right if I take a shower?'

He leaned back against the sofa, regarding her for a moment. She looked spent, he noted. She also looked as though she had been crying her heart out.

'Be my guest.'

How could any man make those three words sound like a prelude to some exquisite pleasure? she wondered with a little shiver, resenting how it made her feel, uncomfortably conscious of how wrecked she looked while he appeared merely dynamically dishevelled, his black hair falling forward, that relentless dark growth beginning to appear around his angular jaw.

'Libby.' His deep voice stalled her as she made to turn back towards the stairs. He was sitting there now with his arm stretched out across the back of the sofa, studying her with a dark absorption, one long leg drawn up across his knee. 'Are you all right?'

His stark masculinity made her throat ache; caused an excruciating knot of tension in the pit of her stomach.

'Sure.' A slender shoulder lifted slightly as she said it. Apart from that she couldn't seem to move. Her awareness of him seemed to have intensified into something almost painfully acute so that it was with a little too much irony that she got past her lips, 'Can't complain. After all, you did promise me some fun.'

Romano made to speak before he realised he would have been addressing her retreating figure. Exasperated, he let his head drop back heavily against the sofa, his thick lashes sweeping down over his eyes.

Was she still blaming him for what had happened when he had taken her to that café? Thinking that he had planned that meeting? Wanted that infernal revelation by Teodoro?

Mamma mia! He dragged a hand wearily across his closed eyelids. He hadn't wanted this to happen. Hadn't wanted her ever to know.

Oh, he knew that at some stage she was probably going to, he thought, but until a few hours ago he had really believed she'd deserved Luca's infidelity; had managed to convince himself that she wouldn't care one way or the other; that she had never cared.

He thought about all she had told him today and about how his parents had treated her. He knew that his father had been a tyrant, and that all but the bravest had had difficulty in standing up to him. But Sophia…

He remembered what Libby had told him about the letters and cards she had sent Giorgio and how they had been returned to her. How could his mother have allowed it? he fathomed, unable to understand it, and yet he knew why. He just couldn't believe that the past could have driven her to treat another woman so callously as to not only rob her of her own baby, but also then deny her any part in his life. And what was worse Libby had thought that *he* had been involved! And now, just when the issues between them looked like being resolved, Teodoro had had to drop that bombshell…

He swore, more viciously this time, punching a cushion in his frustration. He had to get his mind on something else!

But how could he, he reasoned, when every look, every smile, her soft, sexy voice—in fact, the very essence of her—called to something in him that went far deeper than just the sexual? It always had—although that too was charged with something infinitely hotter and more potent than anything he had ever known.

Well, just as he'd thought a moment ago…

He gave a mental grimace as he got up and felt his trousers straining across the hard area of his pelvis. He had to get his mind on something else!

To that end, he switched off his laptop and went through into the kitchen.

At least he could see to it that she didn't starve herself!

Under the cooling spray of the shower, Libby felt her numbing lethargy starting to subside. She felt better for her nap too, since the bitter storm of her emotions seemed to have blown itself out between falling asleep and waking up again, so that strangely now all that remained was a very sharp shaft of hurt pride, with a wearying degree of acceptance and aching regret.

The flaws had been there in her marriage, but she had never wanted to acknowledge them. Luca's lack of real enthusiasm over their coming baby. The constant excuses he'd made about always having to work—and though she hadn't wanted to accept it until now—the lies. He'd spent so much time wanting to go to parties when they could have been enjoying themselves together, or entertaining friends at the castle, when she'd just got back from nursing her dad, pregnant and shattered, having not seen him for weeks.

She'd excused his behaviour as the result of being brought up in a different social circle. Thought that she was the one at fault for not always wanting to join in. She should have guessed, though, she thought, berating herself with hindsight, that the far too easy-going, free-spirited young man she had married would be quite capable of being unfaithful to her without turning a hair. Perhaps she had, she decided now—deep down—and all her efforts at making her marriage work had in fact been for her unborn baby's sake, and perhaps a little because her in-laws had been so determined that it wouldn't.

And that included Romano.

Suddenly, as she let the powerful jets rinse the perfumed lather from her body, her thoughts turned disturbingly to the man who was waiting for her downstairs.

He wouldn't ignore and neglect a woman the way his brother had ignored and neglected her. The woman who caught Romano's interest would have his whole, undivided attention, she decided with a sensually inspired little shudder, unable to dismiss from her mind how sensational he had looked when she'd come across him down there earlier, but particularly the way he had looked at *her*. His concern for her had seemed to touch something elemental deep down inside of her, but it was the way those dark eyes had seemed to lock on to hers that had made the space between them pulse with a powerful electricity. It was the same intangible connection she had felt with him all those years ago when he'd come to see her in the hospital after she'd had Giorgio.

She'd known only subliminally what it was she wanted from him then, but she acknowledged it with total cognizance now.

She ached for his respect!

Did this Magdelena have it? Did she have his tenderness as well as his passion?

Insidiously, as she remembered the way he had kissed her and the feel of those tanned, slightly callused hands moving over her body, that familiar tension began stealing through her blood.

Hastily she threw off the shower-switch, realising where her thoughts were taking her. How could she be thinking about that at a time like this?

It was just the trauma of the day, she decided, putting unacceptable and confusing messages in her head. Yet as she slid her hands over her wet body to swipe off the surplus water, her fingers stilled against her swollen breasts. Her nipples were rock-hard, the rosy buds engorged and sensitive to the touch. Her mind ran riot as her hands closed over them, the dark, dynamic face behind her closed eyes sending messages that were anything but confusing to her contracting pelvis.

I don't want this! I don't want him! she told herself with unconvincing vehemence and stepped out of the shower—to come face to face with Romano, who had just walked in.

CHAPTER SEVEN

WITH ONE ARM still raised to the cubicle door, Libby couldn't move. Her mouth was parted in shock, her bright hair—still swept up—curling damply from the steam, the pale gold of her body gleaming wetly.

'I knocked,' Romano said. 'I remembered that you would need a towel.'

Indicating the fluffy green bath sheet over his arm, Romano felt as if he couldn't breathe. He had thought she would still be in the shower. Hadn't expected to have his senses assailed by the soft perfection of her body and he could feel his own responding to it in a way she couldn't fail to notice.

'What?' Libby frowned and sent a distracted glance towards the unoccupied towel rail, her heart beating crazily in her chest. 'Right.' Was that her voice sounding so breathless, when she should have just taken it, uttered a casual and unconcerned 'thanks'?

Instead she just stood there, her eyes drawn to the deep, all-seeing darkness of his, wondering why she couldn't stop herself from absorbing every detail of his big, hard body, from the bronzed V of corded flesh beneath the open neck of his shirt, down over the rise of his chest and the taut perimeter of his lean waist to the tell-tale protrusion lying against his tight abdomen.

'Is it so wrong to want you?' he asked hoarsely, aware of where her eyes had strayed.

Her free arm came up across her breastbone, felt the reckless hammering of her heart against it. Her breathed, 'Yes,' was barely audible.

'Si?' Head inclined, his lips moved in a wry smile, but Libby recognised a kind of bleak hunger in his eyes.

'You don't like me,' she reminded him, dry-mouthed. 'That makes it next to immoral.'

He moved towards her with the quiet stealth of a predator, his eyes summing everything up. The dilation of her pupils and the flush across her cheekbones; the quickened rising of her breasts with the betraying message in their prominent tips. 'You don't like *me*...' His voice was husky as he touched her cheek, the brush of his thumb across her lower lip sending electrifying sensations down through her body. 'And yet you still want me.'

Libby's tongue seemed to be sticking to the roof of her mouth. How could she deny it? she thought. He was mature and worldly and would know and understand a woman's body the way those first dauntless explorers had known and understood how to chart and tame and conquer. Through sheer skill and experience.

Her lashes came down over her eyes in an attempt to hide the truth, but he tilted her chin with his thumb and forefinger, forcing her to look at him.

His eyes were dark and dense and penetrating, pulling her down into their fathomless depths.

'It would seem, *carissima,*' he murmured as he dipped his head, 'that we are both depraved.'

And if depravity was to want him like nothing she had ever wanted in her life, then she was guilty of it! she thought as his mouth came down over hers, hard, insistent and demanding.

With a small, enraptured groan she leaned into his warm strength, throwing to abandon her last shred of reason as she felt the rasp of his jaw against her cheek, gloried in the full, exciting length of his masculinity and in the graze of his clothes against her wet nakedness.

The towel was still draped over the arm that lay across her back and he tugged it free with his other hand, the friction of the cloth over her bare buttock making her shiver with sensation before he let it fall and brought his hand down to press her lower body into the hard, thrilling evidence of his arousal.

'Romano…'

He trapped her small murmur in the cleft of his mouth. Hers was unbelievably soft, he recognised, from where she had been crying. He ached as he thought about its moist warmth moving unconditionally over his burning skin, and felt the throbbing of his lower body as it hardened in almost excruciating response.

She had just found out that her husband was a bastard and he was taking full advantage of the fact. Somewhere inside him a voice he didn't want to listen to was urging him to give her more time.

'*Cara*…' It took all of his will-power to lift his head and say, 'Tell me to stop. Tell me to stop now and we won't do this.'

She uttered a small moan, her eyelids flickering open. She couldn't have told him to stop if the world had been counting on her, she thought, wondering why he was suddenly having reservations.

He laughed softly then at her hurt bewilderment, seeing beyond it to the desire that burned in her emerald irises, his hands shaping her face, her throat, the slender slopes of her shoulders.

'I know,' he whispered heavily. 'I could not have done so either,' and with that he reached up and pulled the confining pins from her hair, bringing it tumbling down over her shoulders.

'Ablaze,' he whispered heavily, playing on the pun of her name, his hands moving over the flaming silk, his eyes dragging down to where it tapered just above her full high breasts and to the slightly darker triangle at the apex of her thighs that hid the molten heat that was building in intensity between them. 'On fire only for me.'

Her legs seemed to go weak as he pulled her against him, excitement a breathless wanting as his hands moulded her to every powerful bone and muscle of his hard masculinity.

She offered him a tremulous smile as he straightened up to look at her. Would she live up to his expectations? she wondered nervously. Meet the demands of his daunting expertise?

'I'm making you all wet,' she murmured somewhat shyly as her gaze ran over his heavily aroused body and she noticed what she was doing to his impeccable clothes.

He smiled, unconcerned, and said in that sultrily accented voice, 'Then I shall have to lick you dry.'

Suddenly those strong hands that had slid down to cup her buttocks were raising her up off the floor, so that all she could do was bring her legs up and wrap them around him as he carried her through into the cool, serene luxury of the bedroom.

The fabric covering his hard hips was a delicious sensuality against her spread thighs while her head swam with all the possibilities of what he intended to do. And with them her inhibitions fell away and as he sat her down on the virginal white coverlet, pushing her back against it with a gentle nudge, she thought, This is really happening. I'm making love with Romano. With *Romano.* And knew that somewhere, in the darkest recess of her mind, she had always wondered what it would be like.

She thought he would come down to her, but he didn't at first.

Dropping to his knees, he took one of her slender feet in his long, warm hand and lightly grazed the outer edge of the delicate structure with his teeth.

The whole experience was so erotic that Libby gave a small cry of surprise.

'Did you not know you had sensitive feet?' His voice was low, soft, caressing. 'Or did you not realise I would want to taste all of you, *carissima*?'

Her breath coming shallowly, Libby couldn't answer, her whole body tensing in screaming anticipation as his tongue began a long, slow slide along the silken inner length of her leg.

'Romano…'

He raised himself up, following the path of his lips, his dark hair as it lightly brushed her other leg, unbearably sensual on her sensitised flesh.

Breath held, fingers twisting in the bedspread, she lay there rigid, every pulsing cell anticipating the ultimate intimacy of his mouth. But he must have thought it too soon because he didn't touch her most secret place, keeping the tension building with all the benefit of his amazing expertise, using not just his mouth, but also his hands and his voice too now, in a slow, masterly awakening of all her senses.

He said he wanted to taste all of her, and he was doing just that! she realised headily, and through a haze of torturous rapture guessed that very few men would take the time to pleasure a woman in such a way—as though it was the only thing on earth that mattered.

When his lips found the nub of one aching breast she jerked convulsively against him, thinking she might die from the exquisite torture of his suckling mouth. Suddenly, though, she wanted more and, like a brilliant actor with a well-rehearsed cue, Romano moved his hand to cover the swell of her other begging breast, sending quivers of need down to the very heart of her femininity.

He had played this role many dozens of times, she acknowledged with a little painful reminder, but for her it was a first, because not once during her short marriage had she ever been made to feel quite like this—and certainly not since. She had never felt as though she had been made so completely for one man. Knew she never would with anyone else ever again. And hot on the heels of that admission came the burning and intimidating knowledge that made her fingers clench around the strong dark strands of masculine hair they were revelling in, made her bite her lip to stop herself from crying it out.

I love you!

When had it happened? she wondered, hardly able to think. Today? Yesterday? That instant when she had collided with him in the trailer? Or was it before that—long ago—that her subconscious had recognised its soul mate? Recognised it and rejected it, while her heart had been faithful and borne all the anguish and unhappiness in her dedicated devotion to his brother.

She loved Romano and somehow the knowledge had set her free so that when he moved across her, kissing her temple, her cheek, her mouth, the wildly pulsing hollow at the base of her throat, she gave a small utterance of joy and ran her hands down his finely clad arms, tugging at his shirt.

'I want to feel you,' she whispered, made brave by her love.

He gave a small chuckle deep in his throat. 'And so you shall, *mia cara*,' he breathed, drawing away.

Feverishly, Libby watched as he slipped the buttons of his shirt, shrugged it off, tossed it aside. His chest was wide and deep and bronzed, his arms and shoulders, usually made sleek by well-tailored clothes, like velvet over contoured steel.

Drawing herself up to study him unashamedly, wondering what that dark hair feathering his chest and limbs would feel like against her skin, she brought her tongue across her top lip in unwitting provocation, her eyes moving to those long hands as they dealt with the fastening of his waistband.

A sharp gasp escaped her when she saw him naked.

'What's wrong, *carissima*?' His lips curved in mild teasing. 'Afraid I'll hurt you?'

She shook her head, unable to speak, wings of colour spreading along her cheekbones, though she couldn't drag her eyes away from him.

'No.' Kneeling up on the bed as he came back to her, she moved her hands with a delightful urgency over the crisp hair of his chest and the satiny texture of his powerful shoulders, down over the curving steel of his biceps, her splayed fingers coming to rest over the flat, dark masculine nipples. 'You're just so beautiful,' she breathed.

His mouth tilted in wry appreciation as he gently caught her chin so that he could study her. Her magnificent hair. Those expressive green eyes, seductive and yet overlaid with innocence. The soft perfection of her passion-flushed features.

'No woman's ever called me beautiful before.'

He was, though, Libby thought, her whole body weakening beneath his gaze. Like a Greek god, worshipped by the people who had once populated these lands before the forceful determined Romans broke through and reclaimed the region as their own.

Like him, she thought—truly Italian, secretly revelling in her own and far more pleasurable surrender as each of his hands cupped one firm buttock and caught her hard against him so that she could feel the thrilling sensation of his hot shaft against her belly.

A deep groan rumbled from his chest. 'You're the only thing of beauty around here, *amore*.'

His breath bathed her aching flesh as he proceeded to tell her how much, reverting to Italian with whispered caresses that drove her mindless for him until suddenly it was all too much and she heard herself pleading with him, begging, 'Romano, love me…' She didn't know how much more of this sweet torture she could take.

Without wasting another second, pausing just long enough to put on a condom, he tipped her over onto the bed, his crushing weight with his naked warmth driving her into some mindless, sobbing creature, writhing with the anticipation of knowing him completely.

Vaguely, in some sealed-off corner of her mind, she thought of Luca and what she had learned about him today, but it was no more than that. Just one absent thought, because she felt nothing now. Nothing but the need to lose herself in the sound and scent and touch of this one man, in his tenderness and the driving excitement that he alone could provide for her. The past was gone—forever—and there was only her and Romano, here and now.

When he entered her she gave a sharp gasp, but from ecstasy rather than any pain. And then there was nothing but wild sensation as he plunged deeply into her eager body, bringing her legs up around him so that she locked him to her—inside of her—

guided by him in a rhythmic fire dance that built and built in its intensity, until suddenly it splintered into an orgasmic explosion of sensation that went on and on and on, before they finally collapsed together, gasping in the afterglow of its ebbing heat.

She winced a little when he withdrew from her, feeling slightly tender in one or two places.

'What is it?' he murmured, sitting up, concern pleating his forehead. 'Have I hurt you in any way?'

His worried expression brought a gentle smile to her lips. 'No,' she reassured softly and, with her fingers caressing the damp satin of his shoulder, added with a wry little tug of her mouth, 'Just feeling a bit stretched from lack of use, that's all.'

He thought of her first reaction when he had entered her. Although she had accommodated him comfortably enough, she had been surprisingly tight.

'What about…' he couldn't remember the name of the man he had seen her with that night he'd driven over to her apartment, realised with a fierce possessiveness that surprised him that he didn't want to remember '…that guy at the party?'

'Steve?' Steve Cullum was very good at his job, but that was as far as any respect for the man went, Libby thought, cringing, taking a measure of delight, however, in keeping Romano wondering when she noticed the storm-dark emotion…what was it? Jealousy? she speculated, with a wild leap of hope—glittering in his eyes. 'I know you probably think I'm a woman of the world, but credit me with *some* discrimination,' she laughed.

Realising, however, that that sounded as though she would leap into bed with anyone marginally more acceptable to her than Steve, she decided to tell him the truth.

'I've never been one for intimate relationships without some degree of emotional commitment, and I had one of those with pretty disastrous and painful consequences,' she reminded him, thinking of her involvement with Luca and the dreadful price she had been forced to pay. 'It's never been my intention to repeat the experience.'

'You mean…you haven't…' Romano's voice tailed off as he struggled to comprehend what she was telling him.

As well he might, she thought. But then, how could a man like him—a man who had had a stable upbringing, who enjoyed sex as his birthright and who had never known any real emotional pain in his life—understand?

'Are you trying to tell me that you've been celibate…since *Luca*?' His incredulity fell onto a silence broken only by the distant hooting of a ferryboat somewhere out in the bay.

'Don't sound so surprised,' she advised, turning away from those questioning eyes, suddenly ridiculously ashamed of it. 'Some people practise celibacy as a way of life.'

'Agreed, but rarely beautiful young women who are exposed to the public eye and every sort of temptation that would turn most girls' heads.'

She gave a heedless little shrug. 'This lady wasn't for turning.'

Absently he smiled at her rehash of a phrase coined when she was far too young even to remember it. So was falling into bed with him a rebound reaction? he wondered suddenly. A retaliatory response to finding out what Luca had done?

'Why did you change your mind?'

He meant with him, Libby thought, realising she had walked into her own trap. She could feel the intensity of his dark regard inviting her to bare her soul.

Because I feel safe with you!

She didn't say that, though, because she couldn't put herself into such a vulnerable position. Apart from which, it didn't make sense. OK, she might feel as though there hadn't been a minute of her life when this man hadn't haunted her dreams, but she still knew surprisingly little about the deeply private person she sensed he was beneath that invincible veneer. She didn't even know if he was involved with anyone else. He certainly hadn't shown *her* any sign of affection beyond his driving need for her just now, she realised, sitting up. Making love with her was just a pleasant diversion, something that might have happened with any reasonably attractive and willing partner where he was concerned.

'Why, Romano…' through the screen of her lashes that hid a host of painful doubts, she watched the glide of her fingers over one powerfully contoured arm, saying rather coquettishly, 'you should know that you're totally irresistible to women!' And paid for it when he reached up and caught her hand in a merciless clasp.

'Don't play games with me, Libby.'

Of course. He would need her to be straight with him, she thought, her gaze raking over the grim seriousness of his features.

'I—I don't know,' she stammered, unsure what to say. 'Sometimes you meet someone whose chemistry just fuses with yours—and bang!"

A masculine eyebrow arched in wry response. 'Not quite how I would have put it,' he murmured drily, 'though a very expressive description none the less.'

'I didn't mean that!' she protested, flushing.

He chuckled deeply. 'I know you didn't,' he said, releasing her hand to reach up and trace the patch of colour that was spreading across the very photogenic structure of her cheek. 'I just enjoy seeing you blush.'

Dragging his index finger across her kiss-swollen lips, he suddenly let it penetrate the warm cleft of her mouth in such a suggestive manner that Libby felt a needle-sharp response that made that other, more secret orifice throb with awakening desire.

'So…you're steering free of commitment and yet you're happy to make love with me,' he remarked, feeling that part of himself he had thought satisfied stir from the way her warm, moist mouth closed provocatively around his finger. 'Does that mean, then, that you would entertain no qualms about being my mistress?'

Libby's throat contracted in an almost painful spasm. *Mistress*, not *girlfriend*, she forced herself to recognise.

Distracted by the erotic messages she was getting from that wet finger which was now circling the outline of her lips, tentatively she murmured, 'Is that what I am?'

He smiled and stopped the suggestive torment, and began fondling her hair instead, his hand sliding down the rich fiery curtain to where the finer strands tapered out just above her breast. 'You're naked in my bed.' He cupped the soft mound in his palm, felt its instant response as his thumb brushed to and fro across the burgeoning nipple, then with calculated skill dragged his drying finger over the sensitive tip. He saw her eyelids come down, heard her groan against the pleasurable resistance it caused. 'I would not have thought there was any doubt about it, *carissima*.'

And she would be his to do with as he pleased, Libby thought. To drive delirious with his hands and his lips and his voice, pushing her past the boundaries of ecstasy until she was nothing but his sexual slave, ready to do anything for just one gram of his infinite tenderness—for the pleasure only he could provide—because she had been destined to love him.

She wanted to protest, hearing some small voice inside of her trying to warn her that she would only be inviting heartache if she was to continue with this madness. Because it was madness, getting herself involved with Romano Vincenzo. But her body didn't want to listen so that when he pushed her back against the pillows and came down onto her she was already eager for him again, groaning her desperate need into the warmth of his hard, insistent mouth.

She gave a small moan as he moved away momentarily, keeping her mind and her eyes closed as she heard him rip off the condom, quickly deal with another, reaching for him with no loss of desire, her arousal only heightened by the thought of what was to come.

Nudging her thighs apart, he pushed deeply into her wet softness, dragging a shuddering sob from her throat as her body opened for him, taking him in further with every hard, penetrating thrust. And this time their coming together was quick and urgent and yet even more intense than the first, leaving them both breathing heavily from the ferocity of their ungovernable hunger for each other.

He was in the kitchen when she came downstairs, having left her to freshen up alone. He had showered and changed into a short-sleeved white linen shirt and black jeans.

Unobserved in the arched entrance, she leaned against the cool marble pillar, remembering her angry thoughts about him not being able to handle a dinner party, when in fact, watching him move capably around the superbly appointed kitchen, she had to accept that this man—the man she had so foolishly fallen in love with—could handle anything. Including her.

'You like the minimalist look, don't you?' she commented later when they were finishing the beautifully cooked omelettes he had prepared, because every room in the place was starkly serene. From the pale, sparsely adorned walls and dark, uncluttered furniture to the opulent marble, fine mosaics and understated furnishings.

'*Si.* Life is full of complications,' he responded. 'People are a complication. It's good not to have too many—too much detail—in one's personal space.'

And his very private residence reflected that, Libby realised.

'Am I a complication?' she probed, her gaze fixed on the movement of his prominent Adam's apple as he finished his wine.

'*Si*. Very much so,' he drawled.

Why? Because you didn't plan to wind up in bed with me? she thought, with a resurgence of that little voice she hadn't wanted to listen to as she noticed the thin crease between his eyes despite his teasing tone. *Because there are too many unresolved issues between us—like Giorgio?*

'All mistresses cause complications,' she demurred, wondering if there was someone else in his life besides the little boy who might be laying claim to his affections. Like the lovely Magdelena perhaps?

'*Si,*' he agreed, his manner suddenly more abrupt. 'Now, drink up your wine—it's too good to waste—and then, *cara*, I fear I must take you back.'

Guiltily she realised she had lost all track of time, and as she swallowed the last mouthful of the cool white wine, trying to behave as though she was just another of his sophisticated female friends he had just happened to take to bed this afternoon, she couldn't help thinking what a spectacular lover he was and how, after what had transpired between them, her life was never going to be the same again.

And if going to bed with Romano Vincenzo wasn't inviting trouble, she thought, berating herself as she heard his cellphone ring, she didn't know what was.

'It's Giorgio,' he said moments later, with a snap of the small mechanism in his hand, and the grave expression on that handsome face caused Libby's heart to plummet.

CHAPTER EIGHT

GIORGI hurt? Wounded? Just from taking a trip with his grandmother to the coast?

A fall, Sophia had said. While he had been jumping off a low wall. How could it have happened? Libby wondered, beside herself.

All the way back to the mainland she had sat with her hands twisting in her lap, with Romano sitting there beside her, piloting the plane, his face darkly grim.

What was he thinking? Libby wondered now as, still saying very little, he drove them back from the airfield. The same things that were racing through her own mind? That if they hadn't been making love—if they had returned earlier…

Pointless speculation, she realised, because neither of them could have prevented it happening. But if she'd been with Giorgio…if it had been her or Romano with him instead of Sophia…

She closed her mind sharply to that unjust judgement of his mother's capabilities. She was the boy's grandmother—had helped bring him up, after all.

It was dark when they arrived back at the castle and Libby was racing through the softly lit courtyard before Romano was even out of the car.

'Where is he?' she asked breathlessly of Angelica, whom she met carrying a basket of fresh flowers through the great hall. 'Is he upstairs?'

'Giorgio?' Angelica's lined face broke into smiles. 'Ah, *si*. He go straight to bed. He was so tired.' She gesticulated to Libby, looking so happy that Libby wondered if in fact Angelica had been told what had happened.

Romano had caught Libby up before she was even at the top of the stairs. They met Sophia just coming out of Giorgio's room.

'How is he?' Romano quizzed rhetorically, striding past his mother without even waiting for an answer, but as Libby made to follow him Sophia moved slightly but effectively enough to block her path.

'It is not good for him to have too many people around him at the moment,' she advised coolly, her golden eyes raking over her ex-daughter-in-law's dishevelled hair and creased cotton sundress looking for clues, Libby was certain, as to what had been going on. 'He is better than I feared, but the doctor recommended that he should rest.'

'He's my son, Sophia!'

Libby's determination to stand up to her stunned the woman enough into letting her pass. Her anxiety, however, was replaced by shock when she found Giorgio not lying prostrate and in pain as she had feared, but sitting up in bed in his navy-blue pyjamas, grinning impishly up at Romano, who was already sitting down beside him on the bed.

'Oh, Giorgi!'

Libby virtually flung herself down beside him, clasping him to her with a fierce protectiveness for a few gut-wrenching moments before realising that in her haste to do so her leg had collided with and was still lodged firmly against Romano's.

'He's all right,' he said softly, his eyes darkly reassuring, while the child prattled excitedly away to them both in totally incomprehensible Italian. 'Speak English, *mio ragazzo*,' he advised gently.

The little boy obeyed. It seemed he had fallen down and cut his knee and the nice man in the big tent had patched him up and told him to take it easy for the rest of the day.

'Nonna bought me a *big* ice cream—' he spread his young

arms to show them just how big it was '—because she said I was very brave. And afterwards we went to the aquarium because it had a moving floor underneath it and I couldn't walk very well because of my knee. Do you want to see it?' he invited proudly, already pushing back the bedcovers, totally unaware of the questioning glance his mother exchanged with his uncle.

'I don't think that will be necessary, Giorgio.' Romano was restoring the sheet around the child's waist. Beneath the avuncular smile and the weakening relief that was every bit as strong as hers was, Libby decided, she could see the annoyance in the taut cast of his jaw.

'Why did Sophia make it sound as though the boy was lying at death's door?' he complained impatiently, bewildered by his mother's making such a drama out of what had turned out to be nothing more than an unfortunate but natural childhood scrape. 'I can't understand why she had to worry us senseless over something that warranted little more than a sticking plaster. She's not usually given to states of such blind panic.'

Nor would she ever be, Libby supplemented mentally, seeing his mother's ruse for exactly what it was.

'I could hazard a guess,' she said, stroking Giorgio's hair, the words tumbling out of her before she could stop them.

Romano looked at her obliquely. 'Please do.'

She hadn't wanted to, but those compelling eyes were far too commanding, and now, shifting her position slightly so that her leg wasn't so intimately connected to his, she found herself blurting it out. 'She came home and we weren't here. That meant we had gone off somewhere together. She doesn't want me getting involved with you and possibly taking another of her sons away.' She had also probably derived great pleasure from causing her distress, Libby thought, but kept that little piece of speculation to herself.

A line furrowing his brow, Romano stood up, his proud Latin features hard and brooding. 'She's been given no reason to fear that,' he stated.

No, of course not, Libby thought, with a sudden sharp twist of something beneath her ribcage. She had been just a pleasurable diversion for him on a rather—for her at any rate—traumatic afternoon.

'We were out together. That's enough for any mother to wonder,' she communicated to him as levelly as she could, and then, aware of young ears listening, lowered her tone to add, 'Especially if she doesn't like the woman her son is seen to be knocking around with.' There. That sounded careless enough, didn't it?

'I'm not…what is this phrase? *Knocking around with?*' he stressed irritably, slipping his hands into the back pockets of his jeans. 'Some sort of English slang?'

'It means "to associate with",' Libby informed him, swallowing to ease a sudden constriction in her throat as she tried not to notice the dark denim pulling tightly across his lean hips, not at all happy having this conversation in front of Giorgio.

'Ah, that I understand! Well, yes, if what we did this afternoon is having an association, then…' He gave an expressively Continental shrug, his sensual mouth moving in grim acceptance.

'Then you can certainly tell her that she has nothing to fear!'

'Scusi?' Now his frowning bewilderment was aimed directly at her. 'I think,' he expressed with sudden heart-stopping intent, 'that we had better continue this conversation outside.'

More than relieved to do so, Libby jumped up. 'I'll be back in a minute, sweetie,' she promised Giorgio, kissing the top of his head, her heartbeat resuming as a thunderous tattoo as she followed Romano to the door.

There was no one around when they stepped into the subdued light of the landing.

'Now. Would you care to tell me why you're suddenly acting as though I'm your arch enemy?' Romano invited, his tone interrogative.

'I'm not. I…' Libby swallowed to ease the sudden contraction of her throat. What could she say? That she wanted him—loved him!—too much just to be one in a long line of willing females to be notched up on his bedpost? That there was too much at stake to have a crazy, abandoned affair with him and make things even more difficult than they already were? 'I told you…I don't do commitment.' Every syllable was a wrench at her heartstrings, having to turn him away from her like this. But she had to, she thought achingly, imagining how awkward it could get if she was to put herself in a position where—once he had tired of her, as he surely would—it would be embarrassing or even untenable to come back here. And she needed to come back here—and keep coming back—if she had any hope of building a long and trusting relationship with Giorgio. 'This afternoon…I was in shock…because of what Teodoro said. Because of Luca…'

She saw a muscle jerk at the side of that strong jaw, watched some unfathomable emotion cross his harshly sculpted face.

His arm, lifting to the wall just above her shoulder, caused her breath to lock tight.

If he touched her… Even now she could feel her body's response to him in the way her nostrils craved to fill her lungs with his familiar scent, and in the way those most intimate parts of her ached for the sobbing pleasure those lips and hands had wrung out of her back there on Capri. If he touched her she would be lost! she thought.

But, grim-mouthed, he simply nodded, ebony lashes coming down over those incredibly dark eyes as he dropped his arm, leaving her feeling absurdly bereft.

'You're right,' he agreed succinctly. 'It shouldn't have happened, if that's what you're trying to tell me. It's a complication both of us can do without. I should have known better than to take advantage of you while you were in such a vulnerable state. But you can rest assured, *cara*: it won't happen again. You have my word on that.'

He had agreed to it? Just like that? Libby thought, wondering why she was left feeling as if she had been snubbed. After all, it was what she wanted, wasn't it?

'And now, if you'll excuse me, I have other matters to which I must attend.'

He meant confronting Sophia, Libby realised, shaking herself back to her senses to place urgent fingers on his arm as he made to move away.

'Don't tell her what I told you today,' she begged. 'About what happened in the past. Or what I said just now about why she over-reacted. If you do, you'll just give her reason to despise me more than she already does.'

She met the probing darkness of his eyes, felt that fierce chemistry that was as molten as the crater of Mount Vesuvius enveloping her with its heat until she wanted to lean into him, know again, despite everything she had just said, the almost unbearable ecstasy of his kisses.

'I'll do what is necessary,' he said.

The days that followed were relatively uneventful. It was a silent torment, though being close to Romano and acting as if they hadn't shared the greatest intimacy that it was possible for a man and a woman to share, because Romano never referred to it again.

He seemed to settle into a manner of urbane aloofness, born, she decided, out of his controlled yet very real need to have her. He had known what it was like to take her with him beyond the heights of any physical experience she had ever dreamed possible, and was as ridden as she was, she guessed—though for far less emotional reasons—to know that mind-blowing pleasure again. But like her, he didn't dare risk doing anything that could jeopardise the fragile relationship that already existed between her and his family, and having a brief fling with the mother of his adopted charge, and who he probably still believed was a gold-digger, would certainly have done that.

Sophia, too, had assumed, if not a friendlier attitude towards her, then most certainly a more tolerant one, since that night they had come back from Capri, and Libby wondered exactly what Romano had said to her. From the raised voices she heard sometimes on passing a room when he and his mother were together, it was becoming increasingly apparent that Sophia Vincenzo and her eldest son didn't get on, but, as Libby never actually caught anything that was being said, she couldn't even begin to speculate as to why.

Being with Giorgio, though, was pure bliss, and at least went some way to alleviating the tension that seemed to rend the air between her and Romano whenever his uncle was around. And Romano seemed to have made it his business to be around a lot.

He'd turn up at unexpected moments, such as when she was teaching Giorgio a new swimming stroke, sitting on the sun bed, listening to him reciting a poem he had recently learned in Italian—which helped her increase her own knowledge of the language—or hitting a tennis ball back and forth to him on the impeccably kept court.

Then he would come and join in, adding an extra dimension to their relaxation with his charm and laughter, encouraging Giorgio with a role model's praise and easy smile, while Libby found herself stimulated by him at every level.

Because of Romano, she realised, Giorgio's life had benefitted immensely from the paternal influence he might otherwise have been denied, because she was sure that Marius Vincenzo would have had as little patience with an energetic child as she knew he had had with his reckless and impetuous younger son, and she was becoming more and more grateful that Romano had been around to take control.

It didn't take any working out, either, that it was because of his influence that Giorgio's sharp brain and questioning mind was being stretched to its fullest potential. Romano seldom answered a question without inviting his nephew to consider his own solution first, and never denied him a wish without explaining his reasons for any denial. Consequently, Giorgio had all the potential to grow up a well-adjusted and intellectually stimulated child.

'He's been much better over the past couple of weeks,' Romano expressed one day when they had taken a picnic to a spot just outside one of the local villages and were walking back through the narrow street to the large 4 x 4 that he usually drove around the estate. He didn't add 'since you've been here', but Libby knew that that was what he meant. 'We won't know whether his schooling improves until the new term begins, but he's certainly happier in every other way.'

'I'm glad,' Libby said, unable to help adding resolutely, 'And I'm going to make sure he stays that way.'

She felt the glance Romano sliced at her but she didn't respond, calling out to Giorgio, who was cycling along the dusty path ahead of them, to keep his hands as well as his feet firmly on the bike. He promptly obeyed, though too late to take proper evasive action when a little white dog that had raced out from one of the houses ran barking up to him, causing Giorgio to swerve, straight into a stall of meticulously stacked fruit.

'Oh, no!'

As Giorgio toppled one way and the bike and a whole torrent of oranges and lemons went the other, Libby rushed towards him with Romano hot on her heels.

'I'm here. It's all right! It's all right, Giorgi!'

Scooping him up into her arms, Libby cradled him to her breast, feeling the love surge through her as he sobbed convulsively, 'Mamma,' his little arms going automatically around her neck.

It was the first time he had turned to her when he could have chosen Romano. Her hand cradling his head, she glanced over his shoulder and saw Romano squatting there beside her. He had allowed it to happen. He had reached Giorgio first and he could have picked him up, but he had held back. Why? For her sake? For Giorgio's?

A lump as big as the orange she could see lying at his feet seemed to clog her throat. Her eyes, locking with his, were swimming with emotion.

Dear heaven! I love him—so much, she thought. I love him—and he doesn't have a clue.

Shaken and embarrassed by the intensity of her feelings, she clutched Giorgio closer, laying her cheek against his silky-soft hair.

'It's only a graze,' she soothed when she had ascertained there was no damage done, rubbing his sand-streaked knee. 'I think the oranges came off worst.' They seemed to be surrounded by them, as well as lemons and limes, and a showering of dark red peaches too. 'Now do you understand why Uncle Romano and I were telling you to be careful?' A tear-stained little face moved up and down against her shoulder. 'And why Uncle Romano said your little bike's quite big enough for you for the time being?' That didn't produce quite the same response, but neither did he argue against it. Instead, he wound his arms more tightly around her and prepared to enjoy stringing out the last of his sobs.

Watching them, Romano marvelled at how Giorgio had taken to her and, more surprisingly, how easily Libby had slipped into motherhood.

Heaven knew, his own experience of mothers had been tainted to say the least. He certainly had never known the sort of tender feeling from Sophia that he was witnessing in Libby now. Her love for the little boy positively shone out of her. But it had been made clear to him from the start by Sophia—if not in words then with every action and gesture—that he wasn't, and never had been, wanted.

Suddenly he was stabbed by an acute sense of loss—of sudden irrational jealousy and realised it was that lack of maternal affection he was mourning. That bond he could see already building between Giorgio and Libby.

He had wanted to prove himself right. That when he had asked her to come here it was merely for a trial he believed would end when it became clear that she was thoroughly unsuitable to be with Giorgio. That her being here wasn't helping his nephew at all. But Giorgio's eating and sleeping habits, his temperament and his spirits, had improved unquestionably over the past couple of weeks, which presented him with a dilemma he wasn't yet ready to think about as he began helping the fraught-looking stall owner to retrieve her fruit.

* * *

grimaced. 'But then, that's six-year-olds, isn't it? But overall he's very good, if you know how to bribe him into doing what you want him to do. It has taken me some time, but I've learned.'

With every word she spoke, Magdelena was rubbing in the fact that she hadn't been there, Libby realised, resenting this very striking young woman who seemed to be taking immense pleasure from knowing more about Giorgio than she did.

'Yes, well, bribery's never been my strong point,' she told Magdelena pointedly, repositioning the box that seemed to be getting heavier by the second. 'I prefer to use the art of gentle correction and reward to guide a child.'

A dusky-skinned shoulder moved subtly beneath a thin white strap. '*You're* his mother—although I didn't even realise Romano's brother had had a wife until Romano told me. I must say, they kept that very quiet. I've never known anyone like the Vincenzos for guarding their privacy. Or their family name,' she added in a way Libby felt sure was designed to let her know that—supermodel or not—she certainly fell short of the qualifications that were needed to earn any long-term respect within the Vincenzo household. 'I must admit that, when I first met Romano, I thought that Giorgio was some poor innocent foisted on the family because of some...indiscretion. Some unfortunate liaison on the part of the younger brother.' Which was true, Libby thought. Or the unfortunate-liaison bit was at least, as far as her late husband's family were concerned! 'I thought that everyone here—'

'Magdelena!'

The deep masculine voice slicing through the dusk startled both women. Now two pairs of female eyes were riveted on Romano's approach.

The lights had come on around the grounds, reflecting in the pool and casting eerie shadows over the walls of the castle, lending an almost satanic excitement to the features of the man who owned it.

'I didn't realise you were here.' He was addressing Magdelena in his own language. He looked—and sounded—angry, Libby thought, puzzled, feeling his dark presence turning her susceptible bones to liquid. Magdelena's too, she didn't doubt. Because, dressed to kill in an impeccably tailored dark suit, white shirt and tie, clean-shaven, his black hair gleaming in the subdued light, he exuded an air of such untrammelled masculinity it was hard to imagine him doing anything else right then but making love. 'Why didn't you come inside?'

Magdelena looked agitated, Libby thought, feeling almost sorry for the woman as Romano, reverting to English, remembered his manners sufficiently to introduce them both rather curtly.

Keys jangled as he removed them from his trouser pocket and, without waiting for Magdelena to say anything, dictated, 'Wait for me in the car.'

Looking suitably chastened, Magdelena grabbed the keys he was holding up and without so much as a "Nice to have met you" to Libby, made a piqued departure back across the terrace.

'What are you doing? I told you one of the servants would clear all this up.' A movement of his head towards the pool area brought the fresh, vital scent of him impinging on her nostrils. 'There is no need for you to do it.'

There's no need for me to want you either, but I do! It was a lost and mocking sense of hopelessness within her. 'And I told you I wasn't comfortable being waited on. I wasn't born to it as you were,' she reminded him, wondering if he could detect that tremulous note in her voice that sprang from imagining how it might have been if she'd been the one accompanying him tonight, sitting there beside him, coming home with him, having him take her to bed. 'What are you worried about? Afraid I might inveigle you into putting me on your payroll so I can stay here permanently?'

He laughed softly, a sound that made her nerve-endings quiver from the roots of her untidy hair to the tips of her grubby toes. 'What position do you suggest?' His voice was pure seduction. 'Serving me on a domestic level? Or would you prefer something more...personal?'

The innuendo was obvious, causing a swift, needle sharp pain to pierce her heart.

How could he talk to her like this when he was so obviously involved with Miss Snipe-a-Minute Magdelena? She wanted to hit him. Or worse, reach up and drag his head down so that she could taste and feel and savour his hard, insistent mouth; feel the tension in his body as it grew rigid with its need of her as it had that day he had taken her to Capri.

Cheeks reddening with anger and the wild imagery she just couldn't seem to get a grip on, she snapped, 'Haven't you got something far more pressing to do?'

He followed her sweeping glance to where Magdelena was just disappearing into the shadows created by the castle before turning back to her, a muscle pulling at the side of his cynical mouth.

'Some commitments, as you know,' he murmured deeply, 'have to be honoured.'

Oh, and he'd honour her all right! Libby thought resentfully. With his company. His charisma. And then his bed!

Futilely she tried to rid herself of the mental picture of his dark head bent to a full, olive-skinned breast; of those long-fingered hands shaping the dips and curves of a female body brought to fever-pitch for him, pleasuring as they had done so exquisitely with her only a couple of weeks ago.

'You don't have to explain anything to me. I'm not your keeper.'

That cruelly sensual mouth that she couldn't seem to drag her eyes from moved in the wryest of gestures. 'True. But I would have thought you would welcome anyone championing the cause of a charity originally set up in England for the benefit of chronically sick and deprived children and their families, even if it's merely attending a dinner organised in its honour. After all, it was your original concept, wasn't it?'

'*Rainbows in Reach?*' Flabbergasted, Libby stared up at him. How had he found out about that? It was a low-key undertaking, operated through her manager to safeguard not so much her privacy as that of the families of the children she'd been determined to help provide with a holiday of a lifetime. It was what her so-called 'other homes' were for.

The UK-based charity was thriving, but the expansion of something similar in Europe had brought problems when the development company of a small group of villas that had been scheduled had run into difficulties with redundancies, bankruptcies and even fraud rumoured amongst its directors. It had hit the charity hard so that it had looked as though they might have to quell their hopes of extending *Rainbows* to the European continent until an anonymous donor had stepped in just a few weeks ago with his own developers and the pledge of a million pounds.

'*You're* backing them?' Libby whispered as realisation dawned.

'Do you have a problem with that?'

She shook her head, too dumbfounded to speak. 'How did you find out I was the founder?' she said eventually. 'It isn't common knowledge…'

'Any more than was that first hostel you opened for homeless single mothers and their babies with the money my father gave you?' he astounded her further by revealing, chuckling at the shock that was written all over her face. 'I always make it my business to do a thorough investigation of every project I put my money into,' he went on to inform her then, 'but I didn't realise you were the silent benefactor behind the UK charity until someone let it slip last week.'

And yet he had offered his support even before he had known.

A wave of emotion surged through her. Admiration. Respect. And a love so strong for him it was almost too much for her slender being to contain.

He wasn't like Marius. Or Sophia. Or even Luca. He was of a different breed, she thought, recognising it with her soul as surely as her senses recognised the night breezes that fanned her skin and the whistling insects that made such harmonious sounds in her ears. He was like his grandfather. A man of integrity. A strong leader. Yet caring and considerate, too.

Stay here. Stay with me.

Her heart was paralysed with longing so that she couldn't move. Couldn't tear her gaze from those alluring eyes that burned with almost painful intensity.

The sound of a car door slamming dragged her cruelly back to her senses.

Magdelena! Magdelena waiting for him. Magdelena, with whom he was going to spend the evening—and probably the night as well!

'I'll take that,' he said quietly when she made to move past him, causing her breath to lock when his long fingers brushed her breast as he relieved her of the box which was beginning to feel like a ton weight in her arms. 'Now, go and take a long relaxing bath.' His voice was deep and warm and suddenly oddly husky. 'You look as though you could do with some gentle pampering, *carissima*.'

But not by you! Never by you!

She didn't stay for him to see how much his endearment and the sensuality of that accidental touch had affected her, fleeing to her room, where, with her head pressed back against her locked door, she cried with that debilitating sense of loss she had known after he had left her that first time at the hospital, the day that Luca had died.

CHAPTER NINE

'YOU won't ever go away again, will you?'

It was a question Giorgio had been asking since the day his mother had arrived and now, tucking him up for the night, Libby tried to conceal the anxiety that seemed to squeeze her heart.

'What are you going to do?' Fran had asked when her friend had phoned her that afternoon and Libby had decided to come clean and explain about her marriage to Romano's brother. 'Persuade that dynamo to let you have your son back so you can bring him home to England with you? Be sensible, Blaze. He's theirs. You only gave birth to him,' she stressed with a frankness that nevertheless hurt for all its well-meaning intent. 'That counts for nothing in their eyes, I suspect—and you can hardly blame them.'

Now, seeing those big brown eyes looking up at her for reassurance, she smiled and gently kissed the little boy's soft cheek. 'I'll always be part of your life, Giorgio.'

Somehow.

His trusting smile was a further twist on her heart.

'Zio Romano says he might have a surprise for me—but that it's a secret and that I mustn't tell anyone.'

Despite her concerns, Libby laughed, then a little more seriously advised, 'Then I don't think you should tell me, Giorgi. Secrets are secrets because they're shared between two people.

When we pledge to share a secret it means we've made a promise to someone. And you know what we do with promises, don't you?'

'Keep them,' he announced very importantly.

'That's right.'

Gently she ruffled his thick, dark hair, inhaling his clean scent as she kissed him again. She was fortunate, she knew, to have been given this chance to be with him. That Romano had come to find her, no matter how much he hadn't wanted to. So why couldn't she stop worrying that she might suddenly be banned from seeing him again? Have to face the turmoil of endless days and nights not knowing how he was?

The night was drawing in after she finished showering and substituted shorts and T-shirt for a low-cut white camisole and black silk trousers.

Still too early for dinner, she was tripping along the corridor, intent on going downstairs, when she happened to glance out of the window overlooking the courtyard.

Romano and Magdelena were having what looked like a very animated conversation in the softly lit area by the fountain. Magdelena was obviously annoyed about something, throwing out her arms in typically Italian fashion.

Libby had seen Magdelena Moretti here several times since the night of Giorgio's birthday, invited—as far as Libby could deduce—as a guest of Sophia's as much as Romano's.

Now, as the woman made to flounce away, Romano grabbed her wrist and brought her pivoting back to face him. His back was turned to Libby so that she couldn't see his expression, but the two of them seemed to be facing each other in silence for a long moment before Magdelena launched herself straight into his arms.

Libby's hand shot up to stifle a small cry from the pain that was scything through her. If only she could leave here! she agonised, and knew that she would if it weren't for Giorgio. But she couldn't. Not yet! Not until they threw her out. And then…

Then what would she do? she wondered, shutting her eyes to blot out the sight of that intimate embrace. Go back to England? Carry on as she had done before, just living for her work? Existing from day to day? She couldn't! Being torn away from her child now would be like having a limb torn off only worse, because at least a torn limb would heal.

She had told Giorgio she would always be part of his life from now on. She had also told him that it was important to honour one's promises. Which was why she had told her manager on both occasions when she had spoken to him yesterday that she was seriously reviewing her future and her career. If it meant giving up modelling and getting some mundane job—any job—then she would, just so long as she could stay in Italy. Stay near Giorgio…

'They look very good together, don't they?'

Sophia Vincenzo's warm approval of the couple in the courtyard had Libby swinging round. Romano's mother was wearing a particularly satisfied smile.

'Yes. Yes, they do,' she responded quickly, battling to pull her tortured features back in line and hoping she'd managed to sound as though it didn't matter to her one way or the other.

Well, it was true, wasn't it? she thought, glimpsing Romano leading Magdelena out of the courtyard, one strong arm lying across her slim shoulders. They did look good together.

'It would be a merging of two old Italian families if Romano decided to settle down with her,' Sophia enlarged, oblivious to the increasing anguish that was clawing at Libby's insides. 'It is what I've been hoping for. What his father always hoped for. I'll see you at dinner,' she concluded, before carrying on her way to her rooms, leaving Libby to continue her journey downstairs on legs that felt as heavy as lead.

Ten minutes later, sitting beneath the soft lights in the pergola, somewhere in the grounds she heard a car door slam; the sound of an engine starting up.

Romano and Magdelena. Going out for the evening, she

deduced, shutting out the pain of that speculation by trying to absorb herself in *An Appreciation of Impressionist Art.*

She enjoyed art and the book was one she had borrowed before from the castle's extensive library. Tonight, though, the bright colours of the glossy prints seemed to swim before her eyes in a sickening jumble so that all she could see leaping up at her from each page was Romano holding the other woman in his arms, and Magdelena kissing him, shaping his face—hungrily, almost desperately—as though she wanted to carry the impression of it with her for all time.

A light footfall on the tiles edging the pergola made her glance up, startled.

'Is it a good book?'

Romano's voice was as warm and caressing as the night breezes that were fanning her bare skin.

'If you like impressionism.' Her heart was leaping so hard she thought it would jump right out of her chest. Why hadn't he gone out?

'Which you do, I take it.'

He was standing in front of her now, blocking out everything but the strength and leanness of his powerful body casually attired in a black and grey tailored shirt and black fitted trousers. His smile sent quivers of sensation along her veins.

'It's just a glimpse of something fleeting and more real in some ways than a conventional depiction of a thing,' she answered, lifting her chin as she said it. 'Everything's transient, isn't it?' she added with a sadness she couldn't contain. 'Nothing lasts.'

The intensity of his gaze was mesmerising as it strayed to the pulse she could feel hammering in the hollow of her throat.

'I suppose it doesn't,' he said. 'But only because it's constantly being replaced and renewed and so can never become stale.'

'And never stable.' She felt understandably low—depressed—and was trying very hard not to let him see it.

A pleating of masculine brows seemed to indicate that he wasn't entirely unaware. 'You prefer stability?'

Libby shrugged. 'Doesn't everyone?'

He moved over to the cushioned garden seat situated at an angle to hers. Disconcertingly she heard the pale cane squeak beneath his weight.

'In the scheme of things—especially in nature—everything changes,' he conveyed to her impassively. 'The earth. The moon. The sun. Morning. Night. That's why Monet set up numerous easels in his garden. So that he could work on multiple paintings of the same subject to catch the light in all its changing moods. From dawn right through till dusk.'

'Yes, I'd heard that,' she imparted with a fleeting smile, absurdly stimulated from sharing even that little piece of knowledge with him. 'He must have loved what he did obsessively to have shown such commitment. Otherwise he could have driven himself mad and wound up hating it with a passion!'

Surveying her, Romano leaned back, his chin supported by an arm resting on the back of his chair. 'Love. Hate.' Those sensually carved lips twisted almost sardonically. 'Where is the dividing line, I wonder, if one is driven?'

Now he wasn't just talking about art.

The air between them seemed to crackle with a dangerous electricity. Heat radiated through her, making her nerve-endings tingle, her throat go dry.

Caught in the snare of his regard, she lowered her gaze, only to find it riveted on his dark, lean hand. A very masculine hand, furred with silky black hairs and which, with its partner, had pleasured her with a skill that had tipped her over the edge that day on Capri, until she had been sobbing, begging for him, mindless with need.

And suddenly all she could think of was those long hands sliding up under her top, caressing her aching breasts, which, despite everything she had just seen, were already thrusting against the lace-edged silk of her top.

And he knew it, she realised, mortified, reading it in the smile that played around that passionate mouth, feeling that blaze of attraction flaring between them until she felt scorched by its fierce intensity, feeling its molten heat at the secret juncture of her thighs so that she had to do something—say anything—just so long as she could drag herself back from its dangerous spell.

'Giorgio told me that you've got a surprise for him.' Darn! Why had she had to blurt that out? 'He did say, though, that it was a secret.'

'Did he?' Suddenly he leaned over, making her breath shiver from the brush of his fingers as he closed the heavy book that was resting on her lap and relieved her of it with one swift, economic movement.

How had he known she would be here? she wondered, her heart knocking against her ribs. Did he realise that she came and sat in here most evenings after Giorgio had gone to bed? Reading to escape her reckless feelings for him; her fears for the future?

'That's right. But it isn't a secret. Not any longer,' he said, disposing of the book on the low cane table beside him. 'I told him that very soon he might possibly be presented with an aunt.'

'An *aunt?*'

A sister of one's mother or father. Or one's uncle's wife! Like some automated machine her mind processed the information, working it out.

'You're getting married?' Her voice seemed to crack under the strain of saying it, and her stomach muscles suddenly felt as though they were being squeezed in a cruel vice. 'So who's the lucky lady? No, don't tell me! Let me guess.' She was rambling, but she couldn't stop herself. If she had then he would have heard the screaming of her tortured heart. 'Not the volatile Magdelena?'

An eyebrow tweaked almost imperceptibly, but all he said was, 'That sounds as though you don't like her.'

Did he care—one way or the other?

'It doesn't really matter what I like, does it?' she reminded him painfully. 'As long as your mother likes her.'

Surprisingly he threw back his head and laughed at that. 'I do believe,' he said, 'that she has always had great expectations for me in that quarter.'

'Congratulations!' Dear heaven! How could she bear it? Sit here and congratulate him as if she didn't feel a thing? As if she didn't feel as though she was suddenly dying a very slow and agonising death? But she persisted anyway. 'When's the happy day to be?'

'It hasn't been agreed yet.'

'But it's definite.'

'Si.' There was no mistaking the certainty in the deep, rich chocolate voice. 'Giorgio needs a mother.'

She leaped up then, her loose hair burnished by the soft lights in the overhanging vines as she swung round to retort, 'Giorgio *has* a mother! And I don't think I like the prospect of my son being brought up by that…that woman!'

He sat back with both arms curling over the back of his chair now, thumbs hooked into his waistband, the way the action parted his casually buttoned shirt revealing the tantalising shading of hair that furred his chest. 'Does that mean you're objecting to the possibility of my marrying her?'

'*You* can do what you like!' Libby breathed, desperate to keep him from guessing how much she cared. 'It's only Giorgio's interests that concern me. And don't tell me I'm in no position to object because you're his legal guardian—I know that! Believe me, I've never stopped regretting relinquishing my rights to him! But I did! And now I'm expected to sit back and allow that…that patronising *fiancée* of yours…' the word seemed to stick in her throat '…to take control of his life? To *bribe* him into doing anything he doesn't want to do and then give him a pat on the head like some little lap-dog when he does it?'

Rather surprisingly, he laughed again. 'Magdelena does rather tend to look for the easy option where most things—and particularly children—are concerned. However, I give you my word that there will be no bribing or obsequious petting while I'm around.'

'But you won't always be there, will you?' Romano, *please! He's my son. Don't do this!*

She had to bite her lip to stop herself crying it out. He might think that she was pleading with him not to marry the woman for her own sake, and never in a million years was she going to humiliate herself by giving him the satisfaction of thinking that.

The cane protested again as he got up, came over and stood looking out over the poolside, his features as strongly carved and distant as the dusky hills.

Of course he would marry, and marry well. It was just unfortunate that she couldn't stand his choice of wife, and that she felt as though the universe had just collapsed around her.

'I do have an alternative proposition.'

Libby shot him a sidelong glance, her lashes concealing the pained bewilderment in her eyes.

'I think *we* should get married,' he stated phlegmatically.

'What?' His startling statement, delivered as casually as if he were talking about the price of lemons, had such a weakening effect on her that she had to grab the post of the pergola behind her to steady herself. She wasn't sure she had heard him correctly.

'You and I,' he clarified, assuring her that she had.

'But…I—I thought that you and Magdelena…'

'Are not an item,' he responded succinctly.

'But I thought…'

'It seems you do too much thinking, *cara*,' he chided softly, coming to stand only a heart-stopping distance away from her.

'But it's what I saw! In the courtyard. Just now. With my own eyes. You were kissing her!'

'*She* was kissing *me*.'

'Is there any difference?' she retorted hotly, colour staining her cheeks, her pulses leaping in response to his dangerous proximity as she strove to convince herself that this wasn't all some sort of sick joke.

'Magdelena knows the score,' he said.

Which was why she had looked so desperate just now, Libby realised. Because he was probably telling her that it was over between them!

She swallowed, shook her head in an attempt to clear it. 'Are you trying to tell me…you're in love with *me*?' It took a lot of courage to ask him that. But for what other reason, she wondered giddily, would he even be considering embarking on such a monumental step with her?

'Is that what you're expecting me to say?' His eyes were hard and clear and penetrating and, like his voice, totally unfathomable.

'Of course not,' she uttered, hurting, realising she'd been a fool to imagine that his feelings were anywhere approaching what for a few seconds she had dared to hope they might be. The type she harboured secretly—agonisingly—for him.

'If we marry,' he went on in that cool, impervious voice, 'then Giorgio gets his mother back and we…' That hard mouth curled wryly. 'Well, as you so rightly pointed out yourself two or three weeks ago, our chemistries pack a pretty explosive punch—'

'That doesn't make a marriage!'

Beneath the fine tailoring of his shirt his powerful torso stiffened. 'And what are you imagining does?' he suggested coldly. 'The sort of treacly affair you had with my brother? Which proved too cloying for you both when the first test of endurance and temptation came along?'

'That's not true!'

'Don't kid yourself, Libby. If Luca hadn't died you would have been in the divorce court before Giorgio had reached kindergarten!'

He didn't want to be throwing things like this at her. Deep down he knew he was being unfair. She had loved his brother. He wasn't in any doubt about that.

'Your son needs a mother,' he stressed, inexplicably resentful suddenly of her feelings for Luca. He knew, though, that he was going to have to start putting the pressure on if he wasn't able to convince her of the rightness of their being together in any other way. 'I'm offering you the chance to be there on a permanent basis. If you're my wife, no other woman need ever be involved.' And when she didn't answer, too stunned, too bewildered by this whole scenario, he demanded, 'Is that what you want? Another woman caring for your child? Because if it isn't you—then yes, it will be someone else eventually.'

'And if I don't agree to marry you?' Her features were lined. Pained. Troubled.

'I would have thought that was obvious,' he said. 'There isn't any doubt that Giorgio thinks you're going to be around forever. What do you think it will do to him when you force me into the position of telling him that you aren't? In view of the problems he was having before you came here, I think it will do him more harm than good to have a mother who only has time to fit him around her busy work schedule. I won't allow you to walk in and out of his life, Libby. You either go or you stay. And if you stay, then you do so as my wife.'

Of course. The obvious bait with which to reel her in. He knew she would move heaven and earth to stay with her son. But could she achieve that by martyring herself? Marrying a man who didn't love her? Because there was no doubt in her mind now that he didn't.

'Well?' His sensuous mouth curved with the satisfaction of knowing that he had the upper hand. 'Do you not agree that it's the best solution all round?'

Libby turned away from his devastatingly handsome features. For him marriage was a solution. *She* was the best solution. And perhaps he was right, she thought. She was sure that little Giorgio had grown to love her as much as she loved him, and he idolised Romano, while she loved Luca's brother with an intensity that hurt. In different circumstances, she thought, marrying him would have seemed like the answer to a million prayers. Yet now all she could feel was a gaping chasm of longing beyond the dangerous excitement which she knew would only result in her ultimate sexual and emotional humiliation.

'Can a marriage work,' she breathed tremulously in one last attempt to save herself, 'if it's only been arranged to provide a solution to something else?'

'It can—if both parties concerned try very hard to see that it does,' he averred, closing the gap between them, saying with a husky quality overlaying his rich, deep voice, 'Something which I think we should start by attending to right away.'

She wanted to push him away. To tell him that she hadn't given him her answer and that she needed time to consider all its implications, but the feel of his sleeve around her bare midriff was already sending overtly sensual messages through the layers of her skin.

As his other hand slid under her hair and he brought his mouth down on hers, any resistance she might have entertained was wiped away by the hard possessiveness of his kiss.

She wanted this! Had wanted and craved it since she had given herself to him first that day in his villa. She had known then that no other man would ever be right for her, and all she could do now was lean into his hard warmth and acknowledge it fully.

She would be Romano Vincenzo's wife whether her brain wanted it or not. Because it was right for Giorgio. Because, as Romano had said himself, it was the best solution all round. And because, whether she liked it or not, it was written in the stars.

Sensing her acquiescence, Romano groaned into her mouth. His need of her was a throbbing ache pulsing through his body.

This hunger they had for each other was something wilder than mere desire. She didn't know it yet, he realised, but she would. And, with only the smallest gram of guilt to pierce his bubble of success, he knew without doubt that he had been right to push her.

'*Carissima...*' In his own language he whispered his feelings and what it was exactly that he needed from her. He knew she wouldn't fully grasp its meaning and felt unashamedly excited by it, especially since he was just discovering how much those murmured phrases turned her on.

His voice was driving her crazy, Libby thought, while those hands were suddenly doing all that she had been imagining them doing earlier and sliding up under her top.

She uttered a low, guttural sound of wanting as he massaged

her aching breasts. Why did she have to be so weak? she despaired. So feeble?

Yet as he pulled her back against him and she felt the hard evidence of his arousal, her hips ground uninhibitedly against his.

'Romano…'

Her leg moved suggestively against his, the feel of his muscled thigh beneath the smooth fabric of his trousers heightening her own arousal. But when the fingers moving urgently over his chest slid down to his narrow waist his hand slammed over hers, but only so that he could sweep her up into his arms.

'I think, *carissima*,' he murmured above the thrumming in her ears, 'I had better warn the kitchen that there will be two less for dinner.'

She didn't know how he managed to carry her through the house without anyone seeing them, only that he had and that even if they had encountered anyone else, they were far too desperate for each other for either of them to care.

They were both breathing heavily by the time he kicked open the door to his suite—carried her through to his bedroom—and he wasted no time in dispensing of her clothes or his own, or with any further preliminaries. But that didn't matter because she wanted none—only this man, here and now, inside of her.

Mindless as he came down to her, she was already parting her legs for his hard penetration, and she gave a wild cry of abandon as she took him into her.

He might not love her, but she had enough love for both of them, she thought, wanting to give him every part of herself; wanted every part of him.

She had always wanted him.

In the darkest corners of her mind she had known it, even though consciously she would have recoiled from any suggestion of it—as she had with the way he affected her—during those increasingly miserable months of her marriage. The reminder that she might be embarking on another loveless union raised itself, but only for a second, before being obliterated by the driving, throbbing swell of a blinding orgasm.

Much later, as he lay fondling her in the warm aftermath of their passion and telling her, unaware of her misgivings, of his plans for an immediate wedding, he suddenly weighed one firm breast in his palm and remarked, 'You've gained a little weight since we last did this.' Moving his position slightly so that he was lying above her, gently he lifted both breasts in his strong brown hands to allow his tongue to circle first one dark pink aureole and then the other. 'I approve.' His voice was sexily husky. 'I like it very much indeed.'

Libby groaned as his thumbs replaced his tongue in its exquisite torture of her nipples. She had never known them to be so sensitive, she thought, and would have been lost in sheer ecstasy if that realisation, coupled with Romano's comment, hadn't sent shock waves rippling through her.

She hadn't had a period since that first time they had made love, she reflected as his tongue was sliding down her ribcage to prod the gentle dip of her navel. Which in itself wasn't anything to be concerned about. Her periods had sometimes been erratic, and the lack of one this time she had put down to all the emotional upheaval in coming here. Apart from which, Romano had been careful to use protection that day, just as he had this evening. This morning, though, she had woken up feeling nauseous, which again she had attributed to her state of mind. But now that Romano had actually commented on the weight she had gained…

She dragged in her breath, suddenly rigid with pleasurable anticipation as his tongue continued on its rapturous journey and found the tight, tense bud of her femininity.

I'm pregnant! she thought, amazed by how even now—with that shocking possibility—her body was still responding to the slow, warm caress of his tongue. She felt the familiar tingles spread along her thighs, making her breathing rapid, her skin become flushed with building excitement as he tasted her heightening desire. And the second before she was caught up in its throbbing, intensifying swell, she thought, *I'm pregnant. I must be. I'm going to have his baby on top of everything else!*

CHAPTER TEN

'YOU seem to hold some fatal attraction for both my sons,' Sophia remarked unkindly to Libby, clearly disenchanted by their intention to marry. Romano had made it his business to tell his mother while both he and Libby were present, but he had gone now, off to meet the everyday demands of his thriving empire, leaving Libby to fend off the woman's jaundiced snipes alone. 'You do realise, of course, that he's doing what he thinks best for Giorgio. My grandson's interests have always ranked highly among his priorities.'

'I had hoped that you might be pleased,' Libby returned quietly, refusing to give Romano's mother the satisfaction of knowing that she was right as she watched the woman working on her regular flower arrangement in the large vase that stood between the two long windows in the sitting room. 'And we've both naturally got your grandson's best interests at heart.' She chose her words carefully, trying to show Sophia that in no way would her marrying Romano exclude his mother from the role she had always played in Giorgio's life. 'I'd hoped,' she uttered, in a final attempt to secure the woman's approval, if not her affection, 'that at least we could forget the past and try to be friends.'

A sprig of foliage suspended in her hand, Sophia swung round, her golden eyes pained—hard as glass.

'Forget the past? You destroy my younger son's life—and now

you're taking away everything I have left! I might be forced into a position where I have to try to forgive you, but there is no way at all that I will ever forget!'

'Then there isn't any more I can do, is there?' Libby said, defeated by Sophia's refusal ever to accept her as she left the woman to her flowers and went back to her room to make some necessary calls.

Both her agent and her manager were pleased when she told them she was getting married, although they both expressed regret at her immediate plans to become a full-time mum.

Fran, however, couldn't have been more delighted when Libby gave her the news.

'I told you he was behaving like a lover, didn't I?' her friend conveyed rather smugly. 'You tried to deny it, but I knew there was more to that man than met the eye! I'm so pleased for you, Blaze, I really am. I was getting worried that you were never going to let yourself get involved with anyone intimately and settle down with someone. But you couldn't have wished for anything better to happen, could you?'

Only for him to love me, Libby supplied achingly, and resolved there and then that she would make it happen if it was the last thing she did.

Giorgio was ecstatic when Libby and Romano told him later that day that they were getting married and that there was going to be a wedding.

'Can I come?' He was jumping excitedly up and down on the lawn, where he had been playing with the remote-control aeroplane that Libby had bought him for his birthday. 'Please! Please say I can!'

Laughing despite her concerns, Libby dropped down and hugged him to her. 'I wouldn't dream of doing it without you being there,' she promised. 'You can be my page-boy.'

'And will you sleep in Zio's room? Married people always sleep together and then they have babies. My friend Pietro's older brother said so. Will you have a baby? Can I have a little brother to play with?'

The six-year-old's innocent questions made Libby tense imperceptibly. Although as she glanced up and her eyes clashed with Romano's, she saw the line knitting his thick brows before he answered his nephew. 'I think we'd better take it one step at a time, Giorgio.'

Disquieted by his response, Libby looked away. Had he noticed her reaction? And if so, did he think it was because she wouldn't want his baby?

She wondered how he'd react if she told him that she suspected she was already pregnant. She didn't know whether or not he would be pleased. He would probably consider that making her pregnant would have reduced her chances of backing out of this marriage if he thought she had half a mind to do so, although he knew she would do anything to keep Giorgio, so he had to be pretty certain that there was absolutely no risk of that.

What he didn't know, however, was that she wanted his child more than anything else in the world and that—crazily!—she'd feel cheated if the test proved to be negative.

Which just went to show how hopelessly in love with him she was, she realised, despairing at herself as she watched Giorgio flying his plane with added gusto now that Romano was there to share the fun with him, his laughter ringing with a new contentment, his young mind free of the uncertainties that were clouding Libby's. And that had to be worth every sacrifice, she thought.

The ring Romano bought her was a stunning diamond cluster that graced her slim hand with such a mega-statement of everything that was about to happen that she couldn't stop looking at it as they came out of the prestigious jewellery store.

'If you don't stop doing that,' Romano commented drily, with an arm snaking out to steer her round a lamppost, 'you'll wind up with a bump on your head ten times the size of that diamond and the paparazzi will latch on to our little secret, as they are going to soon enough.'

Libby laughed uneasily, her mind still plagued by insecurities, especially since she was hugging a very special secret of her own.

The test she had done the day before had confirmed all her suspicions. She was pregnant with Romano's Vincenzo's child! The unmistakable proof of it, on top of everything else that was going on, was almost too much for her to contain, but she was keeping it to herself for the time being. There was so much to think about—do—what with the wedding—which Romano had wasted no time in scheduling and which was to take place as soon as possible—arranging for the shipment of some of her belongings from England and discussing with her agent and her manager which prospective assignments she could easily refuse and which she had to honour, that telling Romano about the baby, Libby decided, was something she was going to do at some quiet moment when they weren't so engulfed by everything else.

And naturally, as Romano had predicted, the paparazzi got hold of the story within days.

Reporters congregated outside the castle gates. Photographers jostled with each other for pictures of any member of family or staff who happened to come or go, hungry for just one sensational shot of the happy couple.

'Look at this,' Libby wailed when one English tabloid, frustrated by her refusal to grant them an interview, printed its own story, which, true to its usual form when dealing with celebrities, included prying into her previous and very private life.

Under the heading 'Supermodel to Marry One of Italy's Most Eligible Bachelors', it divulged,

...that supermodel Blaze is actually Elizabeth Vincenzo—or Libby Vincent, as she is known in less distinguished circles than the catwalk and the playgrounds of the rich. It's also been revealed that while working as a part-time waitress seven years ago, and

while still only eighteen, she met and married Romano's younger brother, Luca, in a secret ceremony.

There was a short paragraph about the accident, which also included a reference to Libby's father and his connection with the Vincenzo family. '*It's clear now,*' the column went on to disclose, much to Libby's increasing distress, '*that stunning supermodel Blaze is also the mother of Giorgio Vincenzo, Romano Vincenzo's ward.*' There was a whole column dedicated to Romano. How rich and charismatic he was, with words like 'Midas touch', 'billionaire' and 'tycoon' thrown in, along with the speculation as to how much he was worth. '*It seems the lovely Blaze has not only managed to capture one Vincenzo brother, but two,*' the journalist went on to express, '*which could lead some hardened sceptics into saying that this young woman's arctic image is finally melting, and that there is definitely fire beneath the ice.*'

'I don't care about myself, it's Giorgio I'm worried about!' Libby objected bitterly when Romano tossed down the paper after reading the article himself.

'Don't worry,' he advised, although she could tell from the grim set of his mouth that he hadn't read the article with any more pleasure than she had. 'He's resilient enough to deflect any kind of cheap sensationalism that's written about us like this. Besides…' Putting an arm around her, he leaned down and kissed the top of her head '…they'll forget all about us when we're married.'

Which was probably true, Libby thought, but in the meantime they still had to face the clamouring reporters every time they went out, until it was agreed between them to grant one interview to several journalists at the same time, wherein Libby could also make known her intention to quit modelling.

When the day came it was held in the penthouse suite of one of the five-star hotels in a group the Vincenzos personally owned.

Standing there beside Romano—who, in a light beige suit and open-necked white shirt accentuating his olive skin, was dictating the terms of the whole interview with enviable self-assurance—Libby followed his lead, responding to the questions about their forthcoming wedding and the natural interest evoked by the news that she was giving up her career with relative ease.

What wasn't so easy, however, was the much more personal question and answer session that followed, which was suddenly being directed solely at her.

Wasn't she the mother of Romano's brother's child? How had she felt giving him up?

'How would any mother feel?' she answered honestly. 'I was young. Confused. Afraid. But all that's behind me—' she smiled tensely at Romano '—behind us now.'

'Indeed it is.' The man who had posed the question, a rather flabby individual in a casual shirt and creased corduroys, thrust his voice recorder almost in her face. 'In fact, some might say it's a rather fairy-tale ending, especially after the tragic loss you suffered on the death of your fiance's younger brother.' A slight pause while he waited for everyone present to digest this—recall the events of six years ago. 'There has been some speculation,' he went on, 'that your late husband and the young woman who was involved in that accident with him were linked in more ways than just professionally. Would you care to comment?'

Tense lines etched Libby's profile. She wished she'd worn her hair loose to help shield her face from such relentless scrutiny when nausea seemed to rise up as distasteful bile in her throat.

'No, I wouldn't,' she replied, growing sticky beneath the long-sleeved white mini dress she was wearing, wanting to loosen the tapering gold belt at her waist. She sent a brief but meaningful glance towards Romano. 'I'm only here to answer questions regarding myself and my engagement to the present Mr Vincenzo.'

'Of course.' The man smiled, looking like a wolf salivating over a lamb. He had a job to do, she accepted, but, as journalists went, she didn't like him.

'Tell me, Blaze…' he was ploughing on like a relentless bulldozer '…was it love at first sight? I mean, what I'm sure most of us here are wondering—I know I certainly am—is…did that eighteen-year-old waitress who secretly married into such a prestigious family ever give any thought to one day scooping the biggest prize of all?'

He meant Romano, and his intimation was obvious.

At her side Romano's sharp inhalation could have sliced through steel. The corduroy man was looking very pleased with himself, Libby noticed as somehow she managed to drag past a throat clogged with nausea and dizzying distaste, 'I won't even deign to answer a question like that.'

She staggered, felt a strong arm go around her, caught Romano's curt, 'I think we can consider this interview at an end.' A brief nod punctuating that hard statement, he was leading Libby away.

For all his cool dismissal she could tell from the tight cast of his jaw as he guided her through a rear exit that he wasn't that far from losing his temper.

'Good girl,' he breathed above a burst of clicking cameras and a sudden rumpus behind them as his aides restrained one or two determined individuals who would have pursued them. 'Show them a glimpse of fear and they'll hound you for every drop of blood they can squeeze. You handled things brilliantly in there.'

'Did I?' Libby croaked. She wasn't so sure. She couldn't help feeling as though she had made a total fool of herself, unlike Romano, who she knew from experience took even the toughest interviews in his stride. For Libby, though, who had always hated interviews, the whole thing had been purgatory, and now, as he ushered her out onto the roof of the building, where, amazingly, a helicopter was waiting for them, she sagged against him, glad of his supporting strength.

'How are you feeling?' Romano asked as soon as they were airborne.

He was concerned about her. She had been looking peaky for days. Was it the strain of the forthcoming wedding? he wondered.

Was she having any misgivings about agreeing to marry him? Because there was no doubt in his mind that, contrary to what those journalists believed—what everyone would believe when they read the papers tomorrow morning—if it was not for Giorgio, then there was no way that his beautiful bride-to-be would ever have consented to be his wife.

'They make me feel unclean,' Libby expressed as the helicopter soared away over the commercial heart of the city, piloted by the thick-set Miguel, who had been their driver that day on Capri. 'That's how they make me feel. Exposed and vulnerable and somehow…*dirty*.'

'It will pass, *cara*.' Strong, warm fingers linked with hers. 'That's what comes of living life in a goldfish bowl when you really want to be a little mole and hide your head in the ground.'

Despite how she was feeling, Libby managed a wan smile. 'Don't you mean an ostrich?' she supplied wearily.

'Mole. Ostrich.' He shrugged. 'Although an ostrich only *thinks* she can't be seen, while her whole body is still on view to the predators of this world. I'd prefer to keep every part of you for my eyes only.'

Her pulses leaped in response to the sensuality in his deeply accented voice. *I want that too*, she thought, aching for privacy.

She felt laid bare, as though every ounce of guilt she had ever suffered had been exposed and hung up for the world to see. Unclean.

So unclean, she decided after the helicopter had touched down on the landing pad of Romano's island retreat and he was letting her into the welcomingly secluded villa, that she wanted to scrub herself of the awful taste it had left in her mouth; of the blemishing marks that those dirt-digging questions seemed to have made on her skin…

'Oh!'

As she stepped into the cool luxury of his private residence, coming through the archway into the quiet expanse of the lounge, serenity seemed to envelop her in the sights and scents that met her, and which had drawn that wondrous little gasp from her throat.

He had found gardenias. Dozens of them! In baskets. In garlands. In pots. Creamy white and highly perfumed, filling every corner, stand and surface of the magnificent room. And roses. White roses, their scent so sweet as they vied for supremacy with the gardenias and a star-petalled white jasmine, that she wanted to inhale and keep inhaling until her soul was filled with their fragrance.

Everything looked pure and fresh and so beautiful after the unpleasant experience she had just been through that tears pricked sharply behind her eyes. Had he known in advance? Anticipated how ugly she would feel? Emotion almost overwhelmed her, but she kept it in check, her face impassive as she turned around.

'What would you do if you really loved a woman, Romano?' The clash of his gaze with hers made her stomach clench with yearning. 'Someone you believed really loved you?'

His slow stride over the marble tiles accentuated the aching silence. His eyes were fixed on hers with almost brooding intensity, before some emotion tugged his mouth down on one side. 'What would you have me say?'

Of course. What had she expected? she thought as he took her hands in his, stood looking down at them as though studying the vital differences in the dark strength of his and the paler structure of hers. He turned them over, ran his broad thumb across the sparkling ring that bound her to him.

Tell me you love me, please! Her heart craved it with everything that was feminine in her, but her longing fell silently on the perfumed air.

'*Carissima...*' His hand lifted to brush away a tear that had strayed onto her cheek. 'I didn't mean for this—' his chin embraced the flower-filled room '—to make you cry.'

'You didn't. Haven't,' she amended tremulously because he was so unbearably close. 'It's just a culture shock, that's all. The silence...' She glanced past him at the room dressed like a shrine to everything that was pure and honest and untainted by anything the outside world could throw at it. 'The peace...'

He turned his hand against her cheek. It was warm and slightly rough and she leaned into it, wanting his touch, his tenderness; wanting *him* as she had never wanted anyone or anything in her life.

'There is fire beneath the ice, *carissima...*' his voice was a whisper, roughened a little by his need for her '...but only I know how fiercely it burns.'

'Because only you can light it.' She didn't know why she whispered that back. Only that it had seemed like the most natural thing to do as she reached up, touched his lips tentatively with fingers that trembled.

'I know that. Don't ask me how, but I've always known it. The world can rage out there, but it will never equal the ravaging fire that burns when the two of us come together. You ensnare me, *cara*. Enslave me with the silk of your skin.' His fingers lightly grazed her jaw. 'Your hair.' He laid his hard cheek against it, inhaling its perfumed softness. 'Your velvet mouth...'

When his lips touched hers it was with almost reverential tenderness that sparked off sensations in Libby far more intense than any produced by their previous passion.

Sliding her arms around his warm, lean waist beneath the exquisite tailoring of his jacket, her head tipping back to accept the deepening possession of his kiss, she groaned into his mouth, wanting the moment to last, knowing that there was something special about it and that whatever else came her way, or wherever destiny took her, it was something that she would remember all the days of her life.

She scarcely knew how it happened, but one of the white leather sofas had been pulled into service of a sensuously inviting bed and Romano was lying there with her, his kisses unhurried, gentle, his dispensing of her clothes so deftly achieved there seemed to be no interruption in those skilfully arousing lips against her flesh.

'Romano...'

'Hush...' He murmured something softly in Italian and laid a gentle hand across her eyes.

He proceeded to arouse her then, his long, dark fingers blotting out the rest of the world in an incredibly erotic experience, sharpening her remaining senses only to his touch, the sound of his voice and the drugging scent of the flowers.

Guided by him in her blindness, saturated by the infinite tenderness with which he made her his, as he bore her with him to another place, another world, another universe, she seemed to be free falling in a sensual heaven, and suddenly nothing could restrain the sobbing admission that tumbled from her lips. *'I love you! I love you! I love you!'*

She couldn't look at him when, some time later, he got up and moved away.

He had lain there, holding her, for a long time, and yet he hadn't said a word.

Neither had he undressed fully, she realised, watching him with guarded eyes as he tucked his shirt into the trousers he had just pulled on, his features so closed and distant that she had a job reconciling them with those of the man who had just made such exquisite love to her as though he had meant it.

'What's wrong?' she ventured with a queasy little feeling in the pit of her stomach.

'Wrong?' He glanced down at her, a tight, tense smile curving that masculine mouth. 'Nothing's wrong. Why should there be?'

Her loosened hair rippled with the movement of her shoulder. 'You seem…upset about something.'

'Upset?' He laughed then, a sound that didn't quite ring true before stooping to plant a perfunctory kiss on the top of her head. 'You're imagining things, *cara*. Come here.' His hands, still tender, reached for hers, pulling her up off the bed. 'Why on earth would you imagine that I could ever be upset with you?'

She gave him a wan smile, closing her eyes as his mouth claimed and moved gently over hers.

As he drew her close, Libby leaned into him, every part of her yearning for him with aching sensitivity. But suddenly he was pulling back from her, saying with a wry twist of his lips, 'I think it would be a good idea if you got dressed.'

For Libby his urbane yet unfeeling rejection was like being plunged into a tub of icy water. She hadn't intended to reveal to him exactly how she felt. But she had, she realised, humiliated, because it was quite apparent he hadn't welcomed her reckless admission.

She just couldn't believe that any man could make love to a woman in the way he had just made love to her without feeling *something* for her. But it seemed Romano could, she accepted with a hollow emptiness creeping through her. Otherwise why hadn't he acknowledged that involuntary declaration of her love?

Even if she *was* just a proposed bride of convenience, wouldn't it be a feather in his cap and an added bonus if he thought his prospective wife was totally besotted with him? Unless he was totally devoid of emotion, or, she reasoned as the thought occurred to her, he had been so badly affected by some previous relationship that he had shut himself off so as never to risk getting hurt again.

She'd wanted to tell him about the baby too, she thought achingly, stifling a sob. But now was definitely not the time!

Grabbing her clothes, her throat clogged with emotion, she fled into the bathroom, locking the door so that he wouldn't come in and realise how much it hurt.

CHAPTER ELEVEN

IT HAD been arranged that the wedding would take place on Capri. An open-air ceremony in the grounds of the villa. It had also been arranged that Romano would spend their wedding eve there, much to Sophia's grudging approval that it was "bad luck" for a bride and groom to spend it under the same roof.

Not that Libby harboured any superstition about luck—good or bad. She was going into this marriage with her eyes wide open and, while Romano still hadn't expressed any real feelings for her, she was determined to work at winning his love—eventually. Neither had he made any reference to that unintentional outpouring of her feelings for him that last time he had made love to her at the villa. And, though they had made love many times since—in fact, they seemed to spend more time in bed than out of it—she had been very careful not to do it again.

With the wedding only hours away, he managed to whip her into a frenzy of longing with the hungry possession in his kiss before he left that afternoon, claiming as he brought their embrace to a premature end, 'The next time we do this, *carissima*, you will be my wife.'

She was therefore surprised when, later that evening, on her way down to the kitchen to get some dry biscuits to help alleviate the morning sickness she certainly didn't want to contend with on her wedding day, she heard his raised voice filtering out through a crack in his study door.

'I was hoping you'd come around. See it as a sure-fire way of always keeping Giorgio with us—keeping him happy.'

'By torturing me instead!' It was Sophia, her voice, like Romano's, so clear and raised that Libby had very little difficulty in translating what was being said. 'And what would your father, what would Luca say? If you're so determined to go ahead with this…fiasco…you'll not only be mocking their memory, you'll be doing something that hardly renders you fit to be called my son!'

'Perhaps—but then, as you've intimated so many times, I'm not your son! You made that quite clear often enough all the time I was growing up. How do you think it felt knowing you were forced to take me on because my father's mistress didn't want me? Because he was too proud to see his own son turned out into the world with strangers?'

'Is that why you're marrying her? To save Giorgio from having a stepmother? Are you so bitter, Romano, that you don't care about anyone? Your own happiness? Mine? Hers? Just so long as you make me suffer for the past?'

'You're the one who's bitter, Sophia. And what I do and with whom is my business. It's absolutely no concern of yours.'

'It will be if she uses her new position as your wife to try and take Giorgio away from us. Have you considered that, Romano? That your marrying her gives her a far stronger chance to try and sue for custody?

'I see that you haven't,' she went on when no response from Romano was forthcoming. 'But don't try to tell me you love her because I'd find that would take some believing.' Again there was only silence from Romano. 'You can't say it, can you?' Sophia's tone was almost triumphal. 'Because you're incapable of loving any woman. You can't say it because you don't—and I've never known you lie.'

'Since you've clearly worked it out for yourself, there's no point in my denying it, is there? You're right, Sophia. As always. Yes, I want the best for Giorgio. Is that surprising after all I was forced to endure through a double dose of maternal indifference? You're right. I won't see my nephew suffer the same fate. I want what's best for him and to hell with everyone else!'

Libby's hand flew to her mouth to stop herself crying out. She couldn't be hearing this. She couldn't!

'Why, Romano?' Sophia's tone had turned pleading. 'Why must you always do what you so adamantly believe to be right?'

'Goodnight, Sophia.'

Forgetting all about the biscuits, Libby raced back upstairs, her heart striking cruel blows against her ribs.

So he was marrying her solely for Giorgio's benefit! But she'd known that all along, hadn't she, even if she had tried to fool herself into thinking that he did care a little? Yet now she knew the reason for a lot of other things as well. Like why he'd despised her so much initially. Even without believing she was a gold-digger, his view of her would have been soured anyway just for giving up her baby, because his birth mother had done exactly the same thing with him! And Sophia clearly hadn't shown him much affection, Libby realised, if that raw bitterness in his voice was anything to go by. It was no wonder, she deduced, aching inside for him, that he showed such little feeling towards her—towards any woman, his mother had said—if he was so badly scarred by his past.

What was also painfully clear now, though, was why when she had told him she loved him he had chosen to totally ignore it, treating her only with amused indulgence afterwards. What had he been doing? she wondered, fresh pain spearing her as she thought about his unforgettable tenderness that day. Humouring her? Or had he been pitying her? she considered with a stifled little cry escaping her. Dear heaven! She could bear anything but that!

Slipping into her room, she heard the distant growl of his car through her open window, then the throbbing note of its engine as he pulled away.

She would help him if she could. But supposing she couldn't? Supposing she could never reach that part of him that she longed to reach? What then? What would happen when he grew tired of his adoring and convenient wife and his 'best possible solution' for Giorgio? Would he seek more interesting diversions elsewhere?

She wanted to ring him straight away. Confront him with it. Make him fully aware of what she had heard. But her decision to do so—even her angry and hurt resolve to call off the wedding—dissolved under the crushing reality of what such an action would mean.

She would be forced to leave Giorgio if she didn't go through with this marriage and that would be far too great a price to pay. Romano Vincenzo might not love her, but he wanted the best for his nephew and, as far as she was concerned, that was the only thing that she wanted, wasn't it? And then there was the coming baby to consider…

But what about your own happiness? Your self-respect? a tormenting little voice started to nag way down inside. *The torture of being married to a man who doesn't love you?* But she ignored it, because none of those things mattered just as long as she never had to be parted from Giorgio again, did they? she asserted unflinchingly, and managed to convince herself of that—almost.

She awoke the following morning so nauseous that it was some time before she could even think about getting ready.

Fortunately Angelica came in with one of the maids to lead Giorgio away to prepare him for his proudly anticipated role as Libby's page-boy, leaving Libby struggling with her make-up until Sophia popped her head round the door to request the hairbrush he had left behind.

'*Santo cielo!*' she exclaimed on seeing Libby's pale, drawn features. 'You aren't even dressed yet! Are you ill?'

Sophia's eyes were red, as though she had spent the night crying, but after a long night tossing and turning, and then the sickness this morning, Libby was in no state even to think about it.

She had told Angelica she had a stomach upset, which had brought the concerned little housekeeper scurrying back with a glass of something fizzy, which Libby hadn't touched. But after another bout of nausea had sent her darting into the *en suite* she realised, on returning to the bedroom, that Luca's mother wasn't going to be so easy to fool.

'Are you pregnant, by any chance?' Sophia's tired eyes raked over the ivory camisole and matching briefs that gave no indication of Libby's condition. 'Romano said nothing to me.'

'Why should he?' Libby dissembled, flopping down again on the dressing-table stool to try to continue where she had left off. 'I know I'm the last person you would want for Romano, Sophia, but you've no need to worry. I haven't trapped him into this, if that's what you're thinking.'

Had she imagined it? Or did those gracefully slim shoulders seem to sag in relief before their owner turned away?

'Why do you despise me so much, Sophia? Is it all because of Luca?' In the mirror she saw the retreating figure stop—turn around. 'Because he was the only one in this family related to you by blood? Because Romano isn't your natural son?'

A blend of unfathomable emotions crossed the beautiful, matronly face. 'So he told you?'

Libby thought carefully before answering. She didn't want Sophia to realise she had overheard them last night. Besides, in a way, it was because of Romano that she knew. 'Not the finer details.' She put down a little jar of foundation cream. 'What happened to his natural mother? When did you adopt him?' *Whose son is he?* she wanted to know, questions that had been going around in her head all night.

'She was married to someone else, while my husband was married to me. My marriage was in a sense an arranged marriage between him and my father. A merger of fortunes. I was forced to marry Marius to save my father's company. I knew he didn't love me. I even anticipated that he would be unfaithful. What I didn't anticipate was being forced to face the reality of his love for someone else in the shape of their child. Romano's mother was forgiven by her husband, but he refused to keep another man's baby. She was a businesswoman. Totally single-minded. She didn't want him anyway. We'd spent six months in America and when we came back Marius presented me with Romano. No one ever knew he wasn't mine. I couldn't show him the affection he needed—no—that he craved from me. Is that understandable?'

Libby couldn't answer. What was there to say?

'He is very bitter. This is why I told you he only has Giorgio's interests at heart. He will do anything to prevent the boy suffering in the same way.'

Even marrying someone he didn't love.

Anguish tore through Libby, showing itself, she recognised when Sophia said with unusual softness, 'I think you've realised that, haven't you?'

'Is that why you said Giorgio was all you had left? Why you—both of you—bullied me into giving him up?'

A thin smile touched the woman's lips. 'The exact word Romano used when he confronted me about it that night after Giorgio fell down. But you were a mere girl. You couldn't have given the child the things we did—the stable home he's had here.'

'So you took him from me.'

'No.' In the mirror her golden gaze fell, and when it lifted again it held something amazingly close to contrition. 'I wasn't aware of the lengths to which my husband stooped to get Giorgio. But it doesn't matter now, does it? You have him back. And a husband, even though you've probably guessed you'll be left wanting his love. That he can't give anything of himself to a woman—any woman. I know. I've had to listen to more than one foolish hopeful in tears. And yet, knowing that, you'll still go ahead with this wedding?'

'I love him,' Libby said simply.

A spark of something like admiration brightened those tear-reddened eyes. 'And there is nothing a mother will not suffer for her son.'

For the first time Libby felt a glimmer of pity for her late husband's mother, being forced into a marriage with a man who didn't love her and having his illegitimate child foisted on her—startlingly she remembered Magdelena using that word, remembered Romano's reaction—a constant reminder of her husband's infidelity. Losing Luca—her natural-born son—must have driven her crazy with grief, with her grandson miles away in England with the young woman she blamed for causing the death of her only child. That must have made her insanely possessive of Giorgio as the only thing left to cling to. Even so, that didn't excuse her actions, Libby thought. She had suffered unbearably because of the pressure Sophia and Marius had put on her to give up her baby. Especially Marius when he had issued that threat about evicting her father, knowing that she would crack under such pressure—that ultimately she would realise she had no choice. Yes, she had suffered terribly, she reflected. Lost a great deal, though perhaps not so much as Sophia. Whatever else she had to suffer, she thought, steeling herself to meet it, she would always have her son.

'I'm sorry, Sophia,' she whispered, meaning it as she met the emptiness in those golden eyes, knowing that for her, at least, a different kind of torture was only just about to begin.

Heads turned to look at her as, far later than arranged, she stepped out of the helicopter. Now, with a rustle of ivory silk, she took Miguel's arm.

There was Sophia, Giorgio and the little stooping figure of Angelica. Several friends and acquaintances of Romano's. Fran and a few other faces from the modelling world. All gathered there on the manicured, flower-dressed lawns in front of the sweeping arches of the villa, and where live strings played gentle music appropriate to the occasion.

Romano was there, of course, looking, Libby thought with a catch in her throat, more stupendous in his pearl-grey wedding suit, white shirt and tie than she had ever seen him look before. And as he turned towards her, his face a complexity of emotions, his dark eyes burning with a questioning intensity, the ache of longing that rose up in her was accompanied by a sudden sharp wave of nausea so that desperately she found herself praying, *Please let me make it through the service without throwing up!*

He had thought she wasn't coming. When he had seen Sophia and Giorgio arrive, as previously arranged, by an earlier flight, he had been fuelled with excitement and then by an anxiety he couldn't explain as the time for Libby's arrival came and the minutes ticked ominously away.

Sophia had seemed tense and withdrawn. A result, no doubt, of the words they had had the previous night. He had dreaded, though, that Sophia might have said something to change Libby's mind about going through with this marriage, especially after the manner in which he had coerced her into agreeing to it.

She had said she loved him the last time he had brought her here. Cried it out from the very depths of her soul. But other women had done that, only to take another lover the minute they realised he'd been serious when he'd told them he wasn't looking for emotional involvement. It was what women did, in his experience, in the grip of extreme passion. So how could he dare to hope that with Libby it might have meant so much more?

Now as she drew level with him the restlessness that had plagued him for the past half an hour deserted him. Beneath the sleek tailoring of his jacket his shoulders visibly relaxed as he stood, entranced, at the vision that was his bride.

Her dress was the ultimate in elegance. A luminous creation that shaped every line and curve of her willowy body. Small white flowers adorned the blazing swept-up hair that had made her name, her veil just a whisper of lace worn back off her face, which now both shocked and concerned him as he gazed down at her.

She looked pale, he thought, and as fragile as porcelain and, as she looked up at him with a faltering smile curving her soft mouth, he saw something that disturbed him in her guarded emerald eyes.

What was it? he wondered. Misery? A totally painful acceptance of her fate?

'Buon giorno...'

The elderly man officiating had started, his voice deep and solemn over the occasional twittering of sparrows in the trees that hemmed in the villa and the more distant drone of a plane coming in to land at the island's airport.

Somewhere in another world, Libby thought through a haze of unreality. Another time…

Can anyone give any reason why the two of you should not be joined...?

They didn't ask that, did they? Not here in Italy, she thought. Because if they did, would she be honest and utter the words that were screaming through her heart?

Yes. He doesn't love me!

For one breath-catching moment, she thought she had cried it out loud.

Blood pounding, she waited, tension mounting until it reached screaming pitch and she was sure that at any moment someone else would recognise the charade for what it was and make their discovery known.

But the ceremony was continuing—smoothly, without interruption—with everyone oblivious to her harrowed thoughts.

In a daze she heard the man asking if she wanted to take Romano as her husband. She looked at him and their eyes clashed. Did she? Could she spend a lifetime of loving him? Pleasuring him and being pleasured by him—knowing that he might never love her? Was she up to it? she asked herself, the familiar tension that heated her blood giving rise to a sudden wave of dizziness. She had to be, she reminded herself. For Giorgio's sake.

'I do.' She whispered it with every beat of her excruciating love for him, her lashes coming down to conceal the intensity of emotion darkening her eyes.

'Romano…'

Now it was his turn.

Romano's back stiffened. Were they doing the right thing? Was he?

He had given his lovely bride little choice when he had talked her into going ahead with this marriage and until this morning he had begun to hope against hope that she would grow to acknowledge that he had been right to persuade her—that he could make her happy. When she had walked up to him just now, though, the sadness in her eyes had made him feel like a heel for even imagining she would want to spend her life with him if she didn't have to. But then those sad eyes lifted, clear and direct, her soft brows coming together as though querying his hesitancy and the raw emotion that coursed through him fuelled his determination and his escalating desire.

'I do.'

Had he taken a long time to answer? Or was this giddiness that was threatening to overwhelm her, robbing her, Libby thought, of all sense of time?

The man conducting the ceremony was speaking again and they were both following his lead. Then Romano pressed the ring he'd slipped on her finger firmly in place and her fate was sealed.

They were being declared united in matrimony. Libby wasn't sure how much longer she could stand there until suddenly the officiator's tones, lighter now, sounded as though they were coming from under water. She felt sick and extremely faint and everything started to swim in a crimson haze.

She heard Romano's deep voice laced with shocked concern and, from what seemed a long way off, a loud unanimous gasp.

And Giorgio.

Through the swirling mist she caught his anxious little cry and then everything went black as the ground suddenly rose up to meet her.

Strong arms were bearing her into the cool interior of the villa.

'I'm sorry. I'm so sorry,' was all she could say as Romano sat down with her across his lap on one of the white settees. 'I didn't mean to make such a fool of myself. Of you.' Instinctively she knew that they were alone in the room; had heard his deep tones of command keeping everyone else back as miraculously, having caught her, he'd shouldered his way inside. 'I hoped I wouldn't let you down. Let myself down. That I could get through the ceremony at least…'

'Get through the…' His sentence tailing off, he was looking down at her with a darkening intensity in his eyes that made her despair. Was he that angry with her? Ashamed? 'Is it so terrible to be marrying me, *cara?* Is that why you fainted? I felt something was wrong this morning. I knew it! Only I tried to convince myself that what I was doing was for the best. But if the thought of being my wife is so unbearable for you, perhaps we should seriously consider those vows we made to each other out there, Libby?'

Her velvet brows pleated, two dark arches against the sickly pallor of her skin. What was he saying? She wanted to speak but couldn't get her brain to engage her tongue.

'*Dio*! You look like death! And it's all my fault. I was wrong to think I could make this work. To force you into doing something you so obviously didn't want to do.'

'I do want to!' Her voice was desperate. Fearful. 'We both agreed it's the best thing for Giorgio. I want it as much as you do.' What was the alternative but never to be able to share her little boy's life? As Romano had made quite clear to her when he'd proposed.

'But that's not enough, is it?' he challenged. 'I thought it would be, but it isn't.'

Wretchedly Libby shook her head, though in disbelief rather than agreement. She couldn't bear it! Not only to lose Giorgio—but Romano too! Despair as debilitating as the dizziness swept over her. What little colour she had leeched from her face.

She heard someone come in—Sophia, enquiring how she was. Heard Romano dismiss her with reassuring though concise authority.

His attention, drawn away from her for only a second, returned.

'Mamma mia!' Anxiously he caught her to him, the strong planes and angles of his face racked with concern. 'What is it? What's wrong? I'd better call for a doctor.'

'No. It's nothing.' How could she tell him now?

'You fainted! You're unwell. You could be anaemic or something. You've been looking pale for days. It isn't only the strain of entering into marriage with me, is it? Let me help you. For heaven's sake, *cara!* Tell me what's wrong!'

He looked so pinched with worry that she couldn't bear it any longer.

'I've already been to the doctor, Romano. Everything's fine. I'm not ill or anything. I had a particularly bad bout of sickness this morning. It happens. But it's supposed to get better in a month or two.'

'A month...' The line between his dark brows deepened. *'Santo cielo!'* He struck a glancing blow off his forehead. *'Carissima...'* His whispered endearment made her ache with the longing for him to mean it. 'Are you trying to tell me you're...*pregnant*?'

Tears swam in her eyes as she nodded. This wasn't how she had planned to tell him. She had wanted it to be with champagne and candles—with romantic music playing. Not still in her wedding dress, propped up in an undignified heap, looking more like the Bride of Dracula than the blushing variety, listening to her new husband telling her that it had all been a mistake.

'Don't worry,' she murmured, 'I won't hold you to any lasting commitment.' He clearly didn't want that, did he? Any more than he thought she did. For what other reason would he be so ready to let her go? 'This doesn't have to change anything.'

'It changes everything. For heaven's sake, Libby! We've created a child! Doesn't that mean anything to you?'

Her pale features, tilted to his, were lined with anguish. How could he ask that? 'It means everything to me.'

'Then what are you trying to do to yourself? To us?'

'There isn't any "us". You just said so yourself.'

'Only because you're refusing to let there be.'

'What else am I supposed to do when I know you wouldn't be marrying me if I wasn't Giorgio's mother? When all I am to you is the most convenient person to have as your wife?'

'What?' It seemed to shudder through him on a mirthless laugh. 'Where on earth did you get that notion from?'

'It's true, isn't it?'

He whispered something short and crude under his breath. 'You aren't serious?' The black hair moved as he shook his head as though to clear it. 'I can't believe you're actually asking me this!'

'Why not? I tried to fool myself into believing that you were marrying me for myself. That somehow I'd broken through all your prejudices about me, and that you finally...liked me...' she couldn't bring herself to say 'love' '...even half as much as I liked you. But you don't—and it serves me right for being so thick-headed and conceited as to imagine you ever could!' She was ashamed and humiliated to realise that she was actually crying now.

'Carissima...' Those strong, possessive arms were gathering her more closely to him. *'Mia Libby. Amore...'*

'Don't...' She couldn't bear it! Couldn't take those whispered words of love and all that they were doing to her when he clearly didn't mean them. 'Don't try to pretend, Romano. *Please....*' Reluctantly she struggled against his hard embrace, sitting up as he released her. 'I know.'

'Know what?'

'Why you feel the way you do, scared to love. Unable to trust women. I know about your childhood. How your own mother didn't want you.'

Hard lines crossed the handsome face. 'How? Who told you?'

'Sophia.'

Puzzlement darkened his incredible eyes. 'Sophia?'

'Only because I asked her. Because I heard you in the study last night. You were angry—shouting something about not being her son.'

Beneath the pristine jacket Libby felt his hard body tense rigid.

'Why didn't you ever tell me?' she pressed gently and added

what had puzzled her since the early hours when she'd been lying there awake, 'Why didn't Luca?'

Romano made a sound down his nostrils. 'Because it doesn't make for a very pretty story,' he grimaced. 'Apart from which, Luca didn't know. I didn't find out myself until I was fifteen years old.'

'How?'

'Sophia told me herself after I'd found the paperwork relating to my…circumstances.' She could tell from the taut cast of his features how much it pained him to remember. 'I used to wonder why she couldn't show me the same degree of affection she showed my brother. Half-brother,' he amended drily. She knew it rubbed against some raw wound to be opening up to her like this. 'When I was a child I used to think I'd done something wrong. I could never seem to win her approval no matter how hard I tried. It wasn't until Luca died that it really all came pouring out. All the grief and resentment. The whole bitter, sordid truth.

'That day I confronted her about what she had done to you, she told me that after Luca died she intended to leave my father. That it was only his promise to secure her grandson for her that had persuaded her to stay. That was why he issued that threat against your father—although she denied any part in that. Because he was so desperate to keep Sophia with him. Desperate to make amends for all the years she had been forced to care for me.'

So it was the act of a man driven by love, Libby decided, trying not to dwell on the pain it had cost her. Even so, that hadn't made it right.

'When you collapsed out there you made me see that all I was doing was behaving exactly like my father. I was determined to get you to marry me and in the only way it seems the Vincenzo men know how to get what they want—through bullying and blackmail. By letting you believe I wouldn't allow you to see Giorgio again if you didn't. Putting my own desires first, regardless of what you wanted.'

'For Giorgio's sake? Because of the way you'd suffered?' It was a magnanimous gesture. After all, it was her son he was making such a huge sacrifice for, but she wanted to be more to him than just his nephew's mother and a convenient wife. 'Is that why you're prepared to settle down with someone you don't love?' And when he frowned—because of course he didn't know, did he?—miserably she said, 'That wasn't the only thing I heard you telling Sophia last night.'

'What did you hear?' he asked in a voice so low that she couldn't tell whether it was shock or anger from realising that she'd been listening to the whole conversation with his stepmother that made it sound so weighted with emotion.

'You telling Sophia that you didn't love me. That you were only marrying me because of Giorgio. And don't try to tell me I didn't interpret it correctly,' she warned, 'because my Italian's improved no end since I've been back here and the way you speak it is textbook perfect. You said you only had Giorgio's interests at heart and to hell with everyone else.'

Surprisingly he smiled then, a glimmer of sunlight behind a veil of clouds before his eyes darkened again with almost tortured emotion.

'I meant to hell with everyone who would oppose my marriage to you. Not you, *amore.* Have my family hurt you so irreparably that you can't see when one of its members is so crazy about you that he'll do anything—even rip his own heart out, because that's what it would mean to let you go if you really feel there's no hope for us—to make you his?'

'You...' *love* me, she almost said, but didn't trust herself to. 'But you haven't exactly been over-abundant with your affection,' she pointed out, unable to comprehend what he seemed to be saying. 'And after that first time we made love, you didn't even try to touch me again. Not until that night you proposed.'

'Because you asked me not to,' he reminded her gently, although it had taken all the will-power he possessed to do as she had asked, when all he had wanted to do was to declare how she made him feel and have her sobbing beneath him as he took her through the gates of paradise and back again. 'You'd also made it very clear that you didn't want commitment. I didn't want to do anything that would have driven you away from me.' How else could he have got her to respect him? Trust him enough to be able to ask her to be his wife, as he had determined she would be—eventually?

'Only because I was already in love with you. I was afraid of what having an affair with you might cost me—not only emotionally—but also with regard to Giorgio when you got tired of me and wanted to break it off.'

'Tired of you?' He laughed and, catching her hand, pressed it tenderly to his lips. 'That's about as likely to happen as waking up in the middle of another ice age tomorrow. I love you, *amore*. I think I've loved you from the moment I first saw you standing there in the castle with those beautiful eyes proudly defying me to find fault with you.'

Surprise lifted Libby's finely arched brows. 'But you were so supercilious! And sometimes you were downright awful to me! It hurt so much because I respected you—even though I didn't want to—and yet you didn't even appear to like me.'

'I know,' he murmured in self-deprecation. 'But I was in constant turmoil over the way I felt. I thought you were out for all you could get, and yet you bewitched me in spite of it. I despised you for that as much as for everything else, and for making me despise myself as well. When I thought you'd lived up to my expectations in being no good and therefore wrong for Luca, it helped to ease the guilt I felt about wanting my brother's wife. When we met again this time, I couldn't believe how strong the attraction still was after all I thought you'd done. I wanted you and I despised you. For the way you'd treated Luca. Giorgio. Only being interested in money—as I thought. But gradually you made me see how wrong I'd been—on every count—and I wanted you more than ever. I didn't really understand how deeply I felt until I thought you weren't coming—weren't going to go through with this wedding today. It nearly drove me demented. I just didn't dream for one moment that you could ever care about me.'

'Then…you really do love me?' Her tortured expression was beginning to fade, replaced by tears of incredulity.

'Do you think I'd take such a risk on my lifelong happiness by marrying someone I didn't? Risk Giorgio's well-being by having him subjected to the rows and resentments of two people who shouldn't be—don't want to be—together?' The like of which he had experienced through his own childhood, although he wasn't saying that.

'But when I told you how I felt—the day you brought me here after that awful interview,' she reminded him, still having difficulty taking it all in, 'you seemed embarrassed almost, as though it was the last thing you wanted to hear.'

'Because it was what I wanted from you…so much. But you'd put up so much resistance to my proposal, I couldn't believe that it wasn't just sex talking.'

'Oh, Romano…'

'You must admit, *amore*, that there is no passion that burns as fiercely as ours.'

Colour crept back into her pale cheeks as she thought about it.

'And when you looked so unhappy out there today I was convinced you didn't want to be here. You've looked pale and strained almost from the day I proposed.'

'Because I was already pregnant, although I didn't know it at the time and all my symptoms seemed to kick in around then.'

'Ah, *carissima…*' He laid a hand tenderly over the silken-sheathed plane of her stomach. 'I would not have known.'

His hand was warm through the flimsy dress, bringing her lashes down to hide the pleasure it stirred in her. 'No, I wanted to surprise you.'

His strong teeth gleamed white as he laughed. 'Well, you have certainly done that. And now, Señora Romano Vincenzo…' the way he stressed his own name emphasised her marital connection to him this time and him alone '...you will start to rest and take care of yourself and promise to behave as I require a pregnant wife of mine to behave and allow herself to be fully and shamefully pampered.'

Libby laughed too now. She was already beginning to feel better. More soberly she glanced down at the shining gold band on her finger that was a symbol of their love. 'Did we actually manage to complete the wedding ceremony?' Concern etched her slim features as it suddenly occurred to her. 'Are we actually married?'

'Very much so,' Romano breathed, sounding immensely satisfied. 'You passed out just as I was being invited to kiss my bride. If you don't believe me, you'll have to watch the video footage.'

As she had had to do to try and catch up on her own child's life.

'I'm always missing out on the most important and significant things in my life,' she objected, berating herself for it.

'Not any more.' He smiled. 'From now on, *carissima*, you're going to be around and awake to enjoy every minute we spend together. Starting from this very second. And now, if you feel up to it, I think we'd better let our guests see that what I was about to give you wasn't actually the kiss of death but a sealing of our new life together. Our baby's life...'

The warmth of his hand over her middle again brought her yearning towards him as he kissed her, Giorgio running in finally broke them apart.

Without a thought for the exclusive dress, he was clambering up onto Libby's lap, saying in his breathlessly excited way, 'I was scared, but Nonna said you weren't ill, and that I would have to take care of you.' And, seeing that everything appeared to be in order, he asked eagerly, 'Are you really married to Zio?'

Libby exchanged a smile with Romano. 'Yes, Giorgi.'

'Then can I have a new baby brother? *Please?*'

Libby and Romano exchanged glances again, their shared secret concealed behind conspiratorial smiles.

'I'll do my best, Giorgi,' Romano drawled, sending little *frissons* through Libby from the prospect of what he really meant.

And as they watched the child scramble down again and scamper away, because all the excitement and goings on outside were just too much to resist, laughing, Romano dipped his head and gently kissed her again.

'For our new life together,' he murmured. 'And our children's.'

EPILOGUE

PLACING little baby Angelina in her cot, Libby reflected over the past year and decided that she could never have imagined such happiness.

Romano and Giorgio had made her life perfect, and when her baby decided it was time to complete the happy circle Romano hadn't left her side from the start of her contractions until his little daughter popped her head out and declared to the world with a surprisingly strong set of lungs that she had arrived.

Giorgio was thrilled with his new little sister and all his problems had dissolved in the secure knowledge of his mother's and Romano's love for him—as well as for each other. In fact, Libby thought proudly now, his school appraisals at the end of the last term had reported that in several of his subjects he was actually top of his class.

As for Sophia, things had remained a little awkward between her and Libby until the moment that Libby had placed tiny Angelina Vincenzo into her arms.

'She'll need her Nonna—very badly,' Libby had whispered on seeing the tears well up into her stepmother-in-law's eyes. 'Especially when she runs to you if I refuse to let her have all her own way.'

'You're very forgiving,' Romano had remarked a few days later when they left the castle to fly back to Capri. He couldn't believe how devoid of bitterness she was. How ready to share her joy and happiness even with those who had hurt her so badly. 'It's a special gift you have,' he'd said.

She'd given one of her embarrassed little shrugs. 'She didn't have the second chance we did—or the love we share,' she remembered responding.

And now, as she heard his familiar tread on the marble stairs, turned and met the love in his eyes over the bouquet of red roses he was carrying to celebrate their first wedding anniversary, she returned his smile with her heart swelling in response, and knew that that was the greatest gift of all.

They seek passion—at any price!

Three Sicilians of aristocratic birth—with revenge in mind and romance in their destinies!

Darci intends to teach legendary womanizer Luc Gambrelli a lesson—but as soon as the smolderingly handsome Sicilian film producer turns the tables on her, the game begins to get dirty….

THE SICILIAN'S INNOCENT MISTRESS

The third book in this sizzling trilogy by

Carole Mortimer

Book #2758

Available in September